To Jim & Marlene Fisher,

And
There Were Angels
Among Them

Merry Christmas 2006!

Enjoy these comforting stories,

Marlene Bateman Sullivan

And There Were Angels Among Them

Spiritual Visitations in Early Church History

Marlene Bateman Sullivan

Second Printing: April, 2002

International Standard Book Number:
0-88290-694-1

Horizon Publishers' Catalog and Order Number:
1022

Printed and distributed
in the United States of America by

Horizon
Publishers
& Distributors, Incorporated

Mailing Address:
P.O. Box 490
Bountiful, Utah 84011-0490

Street Address:
50 South 500 West
Bountiful, Utah 84010

Local Phone: (801) 295-9451
Toll Free: 1 (866) 818-6277
FAX: (801) 295-0196

E-mail: horizonp@burgoyne.com
Internet: http://www.horizonpublishers.biz

Contents

Part One
A Word About Angels

Part Two
Angels Bolstering Faith

Part Three
Angels Comforting During Trials

Part Four
Angels Healing the Sick

Part Five
Angels Consoling When a Loved One Dies

Part Six
Angels Giving Guidance and Instruction

Part Seven
Angels Were Among Them

Part Eight
Angels Helping People Leave Mortality

Part Nine
Angels Protecting from Harm

Part Ten
Angels at Temple Dedications

Part Eleven
Angels Assisting in Temple Work

Part One
A Word About Angels

This book is a collection of true stories about angels who have appeared to people in the early history of the church, sent to earth by Heavenly Father, who watches over us and is mindful of our lives. The presence of angels in our midst is a demonstration of God's great love for us and confirms His very existence. God appoints angels to teach us the truth, bolster our faith, protect us from harm and to strengthen and comfort us during life's difficult and dark moments. We can all benefit from the presence of these holy beings, whom God sends to protect and guide us. President Gordon B. Hinckley has stated; "How marvelous a gift, that if we live worthy we shall have the right to the company of angels. Here is protection, here is guidance, here is direction—all of these from powers beyond our own natural gifts."[1]

There is much to know about angels, such as; What do angels look like? Are they resurrected beings or simply spirits that haven't been born yet? What part do angels play in our lives? Do these beings have specific duties and responsibilities? This chapter will answer some of the questions people commonly ask about angels.

Are Angels Real?

Although a Gallup poll showed that more than sixty-nine percent of people believe in angels, some find it hard to believe that heavenly beings still come to earth. Elder Mark E. Petersen said, "Many people no longer believe in the ministry of angels. But God does! He has used this means of communication from the days of Adam. Is there any reason why He should not continue the procedure in our day? Those that doubt would do well to remember that God is the same yesterday, today and always." [2]

In 1859, President Brigham Young stated, "Is there communication from God? Yes. From holy angels? Yes; and we have been proclaiming these facts during nearly thirty years." [3]

The Bible is replete with examples of when God has sent holy beings to aid His children, and angels are mentioned over three hundred times in the Bible. Although a few people believe that angels no longer come to earth as they once did, the prophet Mormon declared that angels would always minister to mankind. "And because he hath done this, my beloved brethren, have miracles ceased? Behold I say unto you, Nay; neither have angels ceased to minister unto the children of men." (Moroni 7:29)

Perhaps all that is necessary for us to be convinced of the reality of angels is to do as King Benjamin counseled: "Believe in God; believe that he is, and that he created all things, both in heaven and in earth; believe that he has all wisdom, and all power, both in heaven and in earth; believe that man doth not comprehend all the things which the Lord can comprehend." (Mosiah 4:9)

Angels and the Restoration

The Church of Jesus Christ of Latter-day Saints was brought into existence largely by the means of angels. Joseph Smith, the first prophet in this last dispensation of time, was but a young man when he knelt and humbly prayed to know which church—out of the many that were in existence—he should join. God told him to join none of them, that all had gone astray. Joseph obeyed this counsel and years later an angel appeared, telling him about a book, written on metal plates, that was buried deep in the earth. The plates contained a record of the ancient inhabitants of America and contained the fullness of the true and everlasting gospel that had once been upon the earth but had been lost. The angel prepared the young man to retrieve those plates and through the power of God, Joseph was later able to translate the writing. The translated record became known as the Book of Mormon, Another Testament of Christ.

Finally, the time spoken of by John the Revelator, had come to pass. "And I saw another angel fly in the midst of heaven, having the everlasting gospel to preach unto them that dwell on the earth, and to every nation, and kindred, and tongue and people, Saying with a loud voice, fear God and give glory to Him; for the hour of His judgment is come." (Revelation 14:6)

To those who may doubt that God sent an angel to restore the true Church of Jesus Christ, Orson Pratt gave a simple solution as to how to verify the actuality of that event. He said, "I will tell you how you may prove it, how every son and daughter of Adam now living may know whether there has been a divine message, called the everlasting Gospel, sent from heaven to the inhabitants of the earth by a holy angel. Do the will of your Father in Heaven; call upon His name, and inquire of Him, saying in your hearts: O Lord, hast thou indeed sent forth from the heavens thine angel, according to the prediction by the servant John, bringing to man on earth the everlasting Gospel? If you do this in all honesty of heart and purpose, you may all know for yourselves."[4]

President Gordon B. Hinckley, a modern-day prophet, testifies that angels helped restore the church. He states, "I add my testimony that Joseph was . . . tutored and directed by the risen Lord Jesus Christ and also by angels who were sent from the heavens to restore the everlasting priesthood with all of its powers and keys to reestablish the Church of Jesus Christ in the earth and to set in motion a cause and kingdom that will spread to every nation, kindred, tongue, and people."[5]

A Few Facts About Angels

Through revelation, we know many things about angels. One is that all angels that come to earth either have lived or will live on this planet. Joseph Smith declared, "There are no angels who minister to this earth but those who do belong or have belonged to it." (D&C 130:5) Quite frequently, the ministering angels that are sent to comfort, strengthen, inspire or aid us are our own relatives. This blood tie often provides an extra measure of comfort when we are in need of consolation.

We have also been told that angels reside in the presence of God and that all things—past, present and future—are made known to them. (D&C 130:7)

As for the gender of angels, we know that there are both male and female angels. While many female angels have come to earth, male angels seem to come more often, probably because as priesthood holders, they have more duties to fulfill in regard to church responsibilities.

Angels—A Perpetual Reality

From the very beginning of time, angels have been sent forth as authorized ministers of God to minister to mankind. An angel visited Adam after the fall to teach him about the Atonement. (Moses 5:6) God sent an angel to Moses to instruct him how to deliver the people out of Egypt. (Numbers 20:16) Daniel was saved by an angel who stopped the mouth of the lions who were ready to devour him. (Daniel 6:22)

An angel reassured Joseph, telling him not to be afraid to take Mary for his wife and that he should name her new baby, Jesus. (Matthew 1:20) Angels sang glad tidings of great joy on the night of Christ's birth. (Luke 2:9-14) An angel ministered to the Savior in the Garden of Gethsemane and later, told the two Marys that their Savior had risen from the dead. (Luke 22:43, Luke 24:4-7) Paul testified of ministering angels. (Hebrews 1:14) Spiritual beings opened prison doors for Peter, directed Phillip to a new ministry, and gave very specific directions to Cornelius. (Acts 5:19, 8:26; 10:3-6)

Although we are out of God's immediate presence while on earth, all of the above accounts tell us plainly that Heavenly Father does not leave us alone during our mortal sojourn on earth. Because God loves us and wants us to return home when this life is over, He has given us many aids to assist us in living righteously, such as the scriptures, prophets, the Holy Ghost, prayer and the example of his beloved Son. In addition, God has a vast army of angels that He sends to guide, warn, comfort and protect us during our mortal probation.

What Are the Duties of Angels?

The responsibilities of angels are many and varied. One of their main duties is to act as special witnesses that God lives and that Jesus is the Christ—the Son of God and the Savior of the world. In the book of Revelation, we read; "I, Jesus have sent mine angel to testify unto you these things in the churches. I am the root and the offspring of David, and the bright and morning star." (Rev. 22:16)

The word angel means messenger and another one of their primary purposes is to deliver information to mortals. Often, angels fulfill their role of messengers by conveying doctrines of salvation and important tenets of the gospel to God's prophets, so that they in turn, can teach people correct principles. In the Book of Mormon, King Benjamin was told by an angel what to say to his people. (Mosiah 3:2-4) Angels also directed Nephi, the sons of Helaman, the twelve disciples, and multitudes of others.

Angels are also sent to encourage and support those who have an important work to accomplish. Jesus Christ—at the end of his earthly mission—was strengthened by an angel to be able to endure the agonizing suffering He had to go through in the Garden of Gethsemane. Jesus was then able to fulfill his mission and provide the Atonement as a way of saving all those who would come unto Him. (Luke 22:43)

Mormon teaches us more about the duties of angels, saying; "For behold, they (angels) are subject unto him, to minister according to the word of his command, showing themselves unto them of strong faith and a firm mind in every form of godliness. And the office of their ministry is to call men unto repentance, and to fulfil and to do the work of the covenants of the Father, which he hath made unto the children of men, to prepare the way among the children of men, by declaring the word of Christ unto the chosen vessels of the Lord, that they may bear testimony of him. And by so doing, the Lord God prepareth the way that the residue of men may have faith in Christ, that the Holy Ghost may have place in their hearts, according to the power thereof; and after this manner bringeth to pass the Father, the covenants which he hath made unto the children of men." (Moroni 7:30-32, parentheses added)

Another reason angels are sent to earth is to protect us from physical harm and to defend us from evil. We read in the Doctrine and Covenants: "By mine own voice out of the heavens, . . . I have given the heavenly hosts of mine angels charge concerning you." (D&C 84:42)

Angels can safeguard us time after time in ways we are not even aware of. They can act as guardians to protect us from accidents and sin or as messengers to warn us of danger. Without the protection and direction we receive from the constant presence of the Holy Spirit and from holy angels, the difficulties we face in life would be greatly multiplied.

While angels watch over us carefully, tending to our needs, we must always remember that they do so under God's direction and that under no condition should we ever worship or pray to them.

Exactly What Type of Beings Are Angels?

The term angel can be applied to different classes of beings. Some angels are spirits who have not yet been born on earth. Others are personages who have already lived on earth. Still others are those who have been born and then have been resurrected, such as Moroni, who visited the Prophet Joseph Smith, or the angel who was sent to John the Revelator. (Rev. 22:8-9) Angels who come to earth on official priesthood business can be thought of as administering angels. All angels are God's messengers, whether they are spirits waiting to be united with their body, translated men, or resurrected beings.

Why Can't We See Angels?

Angels are always with us, even though they are rarely seen. Mortals cannot sense the higher nature of angelic beings because our bodies are not finely tuned enough for us to detect their presence. Because our physical body is made up of components of the earth, we can usually only see, hear and touch things of an earthly manner, unless our body is quickened by God. Our mortal eyes are not constructed in a way that allows us to see angels, any more than we can see microscopic bacteria or distant planets.

However, our spirit is composed of heavenly elements and it is through that spiritual part of ourselves that we may be permitted to see, hear and sense spiritual elements. "All spirit is matter, but it is more fine or pure, and can only be discerned by purer eyes; We cannot see it; but when our bodies are purified, we shall see that it is all matter." (D&C 131:7-8)

Parley P. Pratt said; "The elements and beings in the spirit world are as real and tangible to spiritual organs as things and beings of the temporal world are to beings of a temporal state." He explained that to be able to discern beings from the spirit world, mortals must be quickened by a spiritual element and that; "the vail must be withdrawn, or the organs of sight, or of hearing, must be transformed, so as to be adapted to the spiritual sphere . . ."[6] Although our natural eyes cannot naturally discern spiritual entities, God can open our spiritual eyes so that we can behold the finer matter that composes spiritual entities when there is a special need.

What Does an Angel Look Like?

We know that angels are in the express image and likeness of God, as are all mortal men. These celestial inhabitants of heaven can appear either in their glory, having a glorious white light around them—which seems to be their natural state—or as normal human beings. Since angels can appear as mortals, Paul exhorted the Saints; "Be not forgetful to entertain strangers: for thereby some have entertained angels unawares." (Hebrews 13:2)

The angel Moroni appeared in all his glory to Joseph Smith in his home and the prophet described him as follows: "Immediately a personage appeared at my bedside, standing in the air, for his feet did not touch the floor. He had on a loose robe of most exquisite whiteness. It was a whiteness beyond anything earthly I had ever seen; nor do I believe any earthly thing could be made to appear so exceedingly white and brilliant . . . Not only was his robe exceedingly white, but his whole person was glorious beyond description, and his countenance truly like lightening. The room was exceedingly light, but not so very bright as immediately around his person . . ."[7]

The prophet's description of an angel is remarkably similar to the description of an angel given by Pere Lamy (1853-1931), a simple French priest. Lamy stated; "Their garments are white, but with an unearthly whiteness. I cannot describe it, because it cannot be compared to earthly whiteness; it is much softer to the eye. These bright angels are enveloped in a light so different from ours that by comparison everything else seems dark."[8]

In the Book of Mormon, Lehi saw God in a vision, sitting upon his throne surrounded with "numberless concourses of angels." He then saw one angel descend out of heaven and said that "his luster was above the sun at noon-day." Lehi then witnessed twelve other angels and said, "their brightness did exceed that of the stars in the firmament." (1 Nephi 1:8-10)

Throughout the ages, religious art has portrayed angels as having wings. However, wings—as well as halos of light—are merely artistic devices painters frequently use to distinguish angelic figures from mortal ones. We are told in Doctrine and Covenants 77:4, that angels do not have wings, but that those appendages are merely a symbol of power. Many theologians feel that wings were painted to represent the ability of angels to move swiftly between earth and heaven.

Angels in Our Midst

Although angels often appear at history's crowning moments, such as Jesus' birth, the Atonement, the restoration of the gospel, temple dedications, etc., they also come at times that are significant only because of their personal and spiritual meaning in the lives of ordinary but faithful men and women. Most frequently, angels appear in the hour of our greatest personal need, and while such events may have no significant, historical meaning, they mean a great deal to those who are strengthened from the realms above. Most angelic visits occur in a very quiet way and often the only witness is the person who receives needed direction or spiritual sustenance.

Quite often, mortals remain unaware of angels, even when they are nearby and so their assistance in our lives is often undetected. We will never know until we leave this earthly estate, how many times our lives have been altered—without our knowing—by heavenly beings sent to us by a compassionate, loving Heavenly Father.

Few people are privileged to actually see or hear an angel of the Lord, but sight and hearing are only two of our senses. Many faithful followers of God have been blessed to feel the presence of an angel. So even though our earthly eyes may not behold the pureness of an angel, our spirits can sense when they are near. The Lord has promised that if we are true and faithful, the Lord himself may be "in our midst and ye cannot see me." (D&C 38:7)

President James E. Faust once referred to angels that often come to assist us but remain unseen when he talked about the Martin and Willie Handcart Company that was trapped in the mountains because of early snowstorms. Although the suffering of those pioneers was intense and many perished, President Faust said that one survivor stated; "Not one of that company ever apostatized or left the Church, because every one of us came through with the absolute knowledge that God lives, for we became acquainted with him in our extremities. I have pulled my handcart when I was so weak and weary from illness and hunger that I could hardly put one foot ahead of the other. I have gone on (to some point I thought I could never reach, only to feel that) the cart began pushing me. I have looked back many times to see who was pushing my cart, but my eyes saw no one. I knew then that the angels of God were there."[9]

Although all of the experiences in this book relate incidents when people have actually heard or seen an angel, most of the time, the angels that come to assist us remain unseen. But such visits are no less real and powerful. As you read the sacred experiences contained in this book, you will gain a greater appreciation of how closely God watches over us. Every incident in this book stands as a witness that God lives, that He loves us and that He is aware of our day-to-day lives. He knows our joys, he knows our sorrows. The appearance of heavenly beings is a testimony of God's concern for our welfare and assures us that whenever we are in need, angels will be sent to strengthen us.

Notes for Part One

1 Gordon B. Hinckley, Vacaville-Santa Rosa Regional Conference, 21 May 1995.
2 Mark E. Petersen, "The Angel Moroni Came!" *The Ensign,* November 1983, p. 29.
3 Brigham Young, *Journal of Discourses,* vol. 7, September 1, 1859, p. 240.
4 Orson Pratt, *Journal of Discourses,* vol. 19, p. 353, June 16, 1878.
5 Gordon B. Hinckley, "A Wonderful Summer," in *Brigham Young University 1989-90 Devotional and Fireside Speeches* (Provo, Utah: University Publications, 1990), p. 15.
6 Parley P. Pratt, *Key to the Science of Theology,* (London: 1877), p. 133.
7 *Joseph Smith History* 1:30-32.
8 Peter Lamborn Wilson, *Angels,* (New York: Pantheon, 1980), p. 34.
9 As quoted in James E. Faust, "The Refiner's Fire," *The Ensign,* May 1979, p. 53.

Part Two
Angels Bolstering Faith

Angels are constantly engaged in serving the Lord. Part of their duties often include confirming the truth of the gospel, bolstering faith, or reassuring people that they are going in the right direction. In a conference address, Heber J. Grant declared, "I testify that spiritual manifestations are present in the gospel of Christ which we have embraced. Men and women by the hundreds, yes by the thousands, have had visions regarding the divinity of this work, and every honest soul who has embraced it has had the testimony of the Holy Spirit."[1]

God does not hesitate to give mortals a divine witness and assurance of the truth, provided one asks humbly, with sincere faith. Manifestations of the spirit are usually given after a person has spent a considerable amount of time pondering and praying or after they have successfully completed a trial of faith.

Angels constitute one of God's greatest methods of witnessing through the veil. "Wherefore, by the ministering of angels, and by every word which proceeded forth out of the mouth of God, men began to exercise faith in Christ." (Moroni 7:25) Because of this scripture, we know that angels may be sent to reinforce our faith and build our testimonies. Although a veil has been drawn between this mortal earth and the spirit world—leaving each realm to largely dwell independent of each other—that curtain is not impenetrable. Although our world and heaven are necessarily separate, God can grant permission for persons on the other side to make themselves manifest to those on earth.

Naturally, this special dispensation comes according to God's wisdom and desires.

Angels continually work to see that the prayers of the faithful are answered and since God is no respecter of persons, He allows angels to minister to women and children as well as men. "And now, he imparteth his word by angels unto men, yea, not only men but women also. Now this is not all; little children do have words given unto them many times, which confound the wise and the learned." (Alma 32:23) When the prophet Joseph Smith organized the Relief Society in 1842, he told the women, ". . . if you live up to your privileges, the angels cannot be restrained from being your associates."[2]

Because the gospel is the greatest blessing mortals can receive, missionaries are often directed by angels, who help them locate worthy people who are waiting for the truth and light of the gospel. Through prayers of the righteous, angels are permitted to give promptings to mortals. Melvin J. Ballard once explained the relationship between the ministration of angels and missionary work. "Why is it that sometimes only one of a city or household receives the Gospel? It was made known to me that it is because the righteous dead who have received the Gospel in the spirit world are exercising themselves, and in answer to their prayers, elders of the Church are sent to the homes of their posterity that the Gospel might be taught to them, and that descendant is then privileged to do the work for his dead kindred."[3]

The following incidents illustrate how angels come to earth to increase faith and testify of the truth.

"He Received the Knowledge He Wanted"

In 1886, Elder A. Ramseyer and three other missionaries were laboring in Bern, Switzerland, when one of the elders—a man identified only as Brother H.—told how an angel had appeared to a recently called missionary. Brother H. told his fellow missionaries that this prospective elder had been called on a mission to Switzerland but felt woefully inadequate. He felt that his testimony was too weak and his knowledge of the gospel too meager to allow him to leave his farm and go on a mission. Before he could go, this man wanted to know—without any doubts—that he would be preaching the true gospel. To this end, he began praying very earnestly, humbly asking the Lord to bless him with a sure witness and a testimony of the truthfulness of the church.

Elder Ramseyer recounts the rest of the story as it was told to him. "One morning, as this brother was lying in bed, calling upon the Lord for the testimony he so much longed to receive, an angel appeared by his bedside; at first awe filled his soul, but the divine messenger dissipated his fears, and asked him what he desired. The missionary asked him whether this Church was the true Church; to which the angel answered, 'Yes, it is.'"

All of the elders listening to the account quickly realized that Brother H.—the missionary who told the story—was the one who had been honored with that angelic visit. Elder Ramseyer said that when called to preach the gospel, Brother H. was humbly aware of his lack of education but was so honest and earnest in preaching, that he was able to fill an honorable, useful mission. Later in life, Brother H. was called to act as a bishop in the area where he lived.

Elder Ramseyer finished the story by saying; "Why the Lord condescended to favor him with an angelic visitation, is more than I can tell; but Brother H. was an earnest seeker after truth; he received the knowledge he wanted, and he is a witness that Joseph Smith told the truth when proclaiming that an angel visited him; for angels have visited others besides Joseph, as the Lord promised. (D&C 133:36) No church can claim to be the Church of Christ which denies revelations, or divine manifestations; for God is the same today, yesterday, and forever."[4]

"The Angels of God Will Visit You"

Elder Taylor and Elder Bigler served together as companions while on a mission to the Southern States. One night in Kentucky, they were both tired and hungry when they approached a house and knocked. When the door opened, Elder Taylor boldly declared, "We are ministers of Christ sent out to preach the gospel; we desire something to eat and a place to sleep, and if you will give us these, the angels of God will visit you this night and inform you as to who we are."[5]

The owner of the house was no doubt a bit startled at this outburst, but invited them in. After dinner, the elders bore their testimonies to the family and talked about the gospel. Early the next morning, the missionaries started to leave but as they were going through the gate in the front yard, Elder Taylor suddenly stopped. Turning around to face a little girl who had followed them outside, he told her that it was going to storm that day. In the terminology of the region, a "storm," meant a tornado or a very severe change in the weather.

The child went into the house and informed her parents what Elder Taylor had said. Even though the sky was completely clear, with not a cloud in sight, the father began boarding up the windows and doors. Within an hour, a cyclone swept over the area. It completely destroyed the family's orchard but their house was spared because of the precautions the father had taken.

When the cyclone was over, the man hitched up his team and began searching for the elders but was unable to find them. However, Elder Taylor and his companion felt impressed to return to that house a few days later. They were greeted warmly and the mother was said to be "so full of joy that she could scarcely contain herself."[6] That night, parents and children testified that during the first night the elders had stayed with them, their house had indeed been filled with angels.

In addition, the mother told them about a vision she had been blessed to receive. She said that in the vision, an angel had appeared, picked her up and deposited her on a ledge on the side of a cliff. Being six feet from the top, she was helpless to get off the ledge by herself. Her minister stood above, pretending to be trying to help her up the rocky face but actually doing no good whatsoever because the brittle sticks and weeds he held out to her kept breaking off whenever she tried to use them to pull herself up. Then she saw Elder Taylor and Elder Bigler approach.

The account states; "As they came to the edge of the cliff, they extended their hands to her and quickly raised her to the place she desired to stand." Then the preacher left and the angel returned and stood beside the elders. The angel asked if she was satisfied and the woman answered that she was. She woke from the vision feeling a great sense of peace and told her family and the elders that she, "felt assured that her guests were servants of the Most High."[7] The whole family was baptized and many people in the area accepted the gospel because of their strong testimony.

"A Brilliant Light"

Zebedee Coltrin first heard about the newly restored gospel in 1831, when his father, John Coltrin, invited Solomon Hancock—a recent convert to the fledgling church—to his home to speak about the restoration of the gospel. Twenty-seven-year-old Zebedee attended the meeting at his father's home in Strongsville and was deeply impressed with what he heard. Since it was late when the meeting adjourned, the elder Coltrin invited his son and Hancock to stay the night. The two younger men shared the same room and Hancock spent many hours expounding the gospel to his interested friend. The missionary finally fell asleep around 1:00 a.m. but Zebedee could not put the words he had heard out of his mind. Long after 2:00 a.m., Zebedee lay awake, reflecting deeply on all that had been said. Finally he made a decision.

Zebedee recorded in his journal; "Thinking on what I had heard, I resolved to be baptized and as I lay meditating, the room became lighted up with a brilliant light and I saw a number of men dressed in white robes, like unto what we call temple clothes. Soon after the vision closed."[8] This experience was proof to Zebedee that being baptized was the right course of action and that God was pleased with his decision to join the church.

The next morning, on January 9, 1831, Zebedee asked Solomon Hancock to baptize him. It was a frigid day and the ice that covered the nearby body of water was a foot thick. The men brought out their axes and chopped a hole in the ice so that the ordinance could be performed. Zebedee stated that the cold did not bother him at all, as he was warmed with the fervor of his newfound faith. After his conversion, Zebedee became a great friend and stalwart supporter of the Prophet Joseph Smith and served many years as a leader in the church.

"It Is Only Proper That You Receive a Witness"

Mary Whitmer—or as she was most often called, Mother Whitmer—was allowed to see not only an angel but the golden plates as well—the only woman on earth accorded that special privilege.

Prior to Mary's experience, Joseph Smith was working hard to translate the Book of Mormon but he was constantly being interrupted by intense persecution. The work was proceeding very slowly until he and Emma, along with Oliver Cowdery, were invited to stay at the Whitmer home—a quiet haven where the translating could move along more quickly. Having so many guests was a great burden on Mother

Whitmer, but she never complained. Because of her faithfulness and patient acceptance of additional labor, Mother Whitmer had a special witness given to her one spring day.

Shortly before her experience with an angel, her son David left for Harmony to pick up Joseph and Oliver, who were just returning from a trip to Pennsylvania. The three men were nearly home when a pleasant-looking old man suddenly appeared in the road. They pulled up, greeted him and David asked if the man was going their way and wanted a ride. The gentleman declined, saying he was going to Cumorah. David was puzzled. He had never heard of such a place. David looked curiously at Joseph, to see what the prophet made of such a strange name, then to Oliver. When he turned back to look at the traveler, the man had disappeared.

Joseph, looking gently amused, asked a bewildered David to describe the man in detail. David recalled that the man had been five feet, nine inches tall, heavy-set, dressed in a suit of brown woolen clothes and had white hair and a beard. He added that the man had a sort of knapsack on his back with something in it that was shaped like a book.

When the men arrived home, Mother Whitmer told them about her angelic experience, which David later related as follows:

"My mother was going to milk the cows, when she was met out near the yard by the same old man (judging by her description of him), who said to her: 'You have been very faithful and diligent in your labors, but you are tired because of the increase in your toil; it is proper, therefore, that you should receive a witness that your faith may be strengthened.' Thereupon he showed her the plates. My father and mother had a large family of their own, the addition to it, therefore, of Joseph, his wife Emma and Oliver very greatly increased the toil and anxiety of my mother. And although she had never complained she had sometimes felt that her labor was too much, or at least she was perhaps beginning to feel so. This circumstance, however, completely removed all such feelings and nerved her up for her increased responsibilities."[9]

"I Saw Angels With the Book of Mormon"

An investigator of the early church, Zera Pulsipher, received not one, but two, angelic witnesses from heaven. One was regarding the truth of the gospel and the second was to console him as to his wife's well being after she had passed away.

Zera was born June 24, 1789 in Rockingham, Vermont. When he was twenty-one years old, he fell in love with and married Mary Randall. However, their time together on earth was cut short when—after only one year of marriage—she died. Zera had not heard about the Church of Jesus Christ and after losing his young wife, felt uneasy and troubled about Mary's circumstances. He prayed diligently to be able to find out if all was well with her. His desires were granted when Mary appeared to him, although at the time—not being familiar with the church—he must have been puzzled by her reference to Zion. Later, however, when he learned about the church, many things regarding his wife's visit became clear.

After he joined the church, Zera wrote about Mary's appearance: "After her death I had some anxiety about her state and condition; consequently, in answer to my desires, she came to me in vision and appearing natural, looked pleasant as ever she did and sat down by my side and assisted me in singing a hymn beginning thus: 'That glorious day is drawing nigh when Zion's light shall shine.' This she did with seeming composure. This vision took all my anxiety concerning her in-as-much as she seemed to enjoy herself well. The hymn which she introduced and sang with me applied to the last great work of the last dispensation of the fullness of times."[10]

In 1814, after his wife's death, Zera moved to Onondaga County in New York. He remarried and built a mill, which he ran with his brother. After the Book of Mormon was printed, a copy made its way to town. Zera borrowed the book and after carefully reading it through twice, believed it was true. He began investigating the church and prayed to know whether the new religion was true or not. Zera then received a witness. He wrote about his experience in his journal.

"One day I was thrashing in my barn with the doors shut. All at once there seemed to be a ray of light from heaven which caused me to stop work for a short time, but I soon began it (sic) again. Then in a few minutes another light came over my head which caused me to look up. I thought I saw angels with the book of Mormon in their hands in the attitude of showing it to me and saying 'This is the great revelation of the last days in which all things spoken of by the prophets shall be fulfilled.' The vision was so open and plain that I began to rejoice exceedingly so that I walked the length of my barn crying, 'Glory, Hallelujah to God and the Lamb forever.'

"For some time it seemed a little difficult to keep my mind in a reasonable state of order, I was so filled with the joys of heaven. But when my mind became calm I called the church together (I was their minister) and informed them of what I had seen. I told them of my determination to join the Church of latter-day Saints, which I did and a large body of my church went with me. I was ordained to the office of Elder and went to preaching with considerable success at home and abroad. I had the privilege of baptizing Wilford Woodruff on the 31st of December 1833 at Richland, New York."[11]

After his baptism in the fall of 1831, Zera bore a firm testimony about the truth of the gospel to his friends in the Baptist Church. Many accepted the gospel's message on the strength of Zera's convictions and were baptized into The Church of Jesus Christ of Latter-day Saints.

"Don't You Remember Our Agreement?"

In the late 1870s, diphtheria began raging in Utah's Sanpete County. After seeing a number of their friends and relatives die, two young boys had a solemn discussion about death. While sitting in an apple orchard, the two friends, Tony (Anton) Nielson and P.C. Anderson discussed the idea of life beyond the grave. The boys came to the conclusion that in order to truly know what life was like in the next life, a person would have to talk with someone who lived there. Since both boys believed in life after death, they decided to make a pact. Holding hands solemnly, Tony and P.C. made a commitment to each other, saying, "Let us enter into an agreement that, if it is possible, the one of us who dies first shall come and tell the other his condition in the spirit world."[12] A third boy, Joseph Hansen, witnessed this solemn contract.

Months and years passed and the boys became teenagers. Then Tony died, just two weeks before his eighteenth birthday. Nine months later, Tony's father heard a rumor that someone had seen his dead son and began tracing it down to discover the source. It took some time to find out that the person who claimed to have seen his son was P.C. Anderson, his son's old friend. Knowing that Anderson was a truthful and strictly upright man, Brother Nielson went to see him. The still grieving father asked if the rumors were true. Had Anderson actually seen Tony since his death?

Anderson replied, "Yes. It was about nine months after Anton's death. I was irrigating one day south-west of town. Having changed the course of the stream, I walked a short distance over to the road, where I sat down, partly lying or reclining on my side. While in that position, and looking straight in the direction I was facing, I saw Tony walking right up to me, as naturally as I ever saw him in my life. Not having the least fear, and entirely forgetting myself at the moment, I said: 'Why, Tony, I thought you were dead.' He looked me straight in the face and answered: 'Don't you remember our agreement?'

"Hesitatingly, I said, 'Yes, but I thought you were dead.'

"He more sternly inquired again: 'Don't you remember our agreement?'

"A third time I remarked, 'Yes but I thought you were dead. Then how came you here, and what are your conditions?' I added.

"If it had not been for that agreement,' he answered, 'I should not have been permitted to come here. It has been very difficult and hard for me to come. I am very busy, have a great deal to do; and my conditions are more excellent than you are able to comprehend.' At that very moment he disappeared before my eyes, apparently being in a great hurry."[13]

Brother Nielson then asked if Anderson could have been asleep at the time. When Anderson assured him that he had been wide awake, Brother Nielson became convinced that it was a true visitation. He went on to say that he could not believe Anderson's experience any more than if it had happened to himself, since Anderson had a wide reputation as a morally upright man and was quite prominent in the community.

"You Shall Have Eternal Life"

Caroline A. Joyce received the rare blessing of having an angel speak to her. Caroline was living in Boston, Massachusetts when she heard about a strange sect that professed to believe in the same gospel that was taught by Jesus Christ. When Caroline found out that missionaries from this new church were holding a meeting in Boylston Hall, she decided to attend. Elder Erastus Snow spoke and as Caroline listened to his words, she said, "His words were like unto a song heard in my far off childhood, once forgotten but now returning afresh to my memory, and I cried for very joy."[14]

However, her happiness was short-lived. When Caroline went home to tell her parents the good news about God's church being restored to earth, they thought she was insane. Speaking out loud—as if Caroline was invisible—her parents discussed what to do about their daughter's 'condition.' Later, when Caroline asked if she could be baptized, her father told her that if she joined with the Mormons, she would have to leave their home. After some contemplation, Caroline decided to be baptized but was filled with regret about disobeying her parents. Fortunately, her parents relented and Caroline was allowed to stay in her home, although her mother continued to try to persuade her to leave the church.

Caroline then had an experience that greatly strengthened her testimony. She said, "One night I had been to meeting where the Spirit of God seemed to fill the house, and returned home thankful to my Heavenly Father that I ever heard the Gospel. I laid down to rest beside my mother, who commenced upbraiding me, and instantly I was filled with remorse that I was the cause of her unhappiness. I did not know what to say and was hesitating when, just over my head, a voice, not in a whisper, but still and low, said these words: 'If you will leave father and mother, you shall have eternal life.' I asked, 'Mother, did you hear that?' She answered, 'You are bewitched!'"

"I knew then she had not heard the voice, but my mind was at rest and I went to sleep. I have heard the same voice since, not in dreams, but in daylight, when in trouble and uncertain which way to go; and I know God lives and guides this people called 'Mormons.' I know also the gifts and blessings are in The Church of Jesus Christ of Latter-day Saints, and that same faith once delivered to the Saints is also ours, if we live for it."[15]

"I Know You!"

Elder Tom Shreeve was sailing to New Zealand on the ship, the Wakatipu, to preach the gospel, when he saw the spirit of a woman on board. He relates; ". . . I lay wide-awake and comfortable in my berth—lulled by the swirl of waters against the ship—I saw, standing on a step-ladder by the side of my berth and looking down upon me, a little old lady. She was short and stout, and pleasant-looking. Her eyes gleamed with kindness, and she smiled in a most friendly fashion. How she came there I knew not, but she seemed to feel perfectly at home. When my eyes met hers, she began to nod at me. She continued her droll recognition for several moments, and then she spoke in a jolly tone:

"'I know you; I know you! And you shall know me when we meet again.' Then she disappeared as suddenly as she had come. But her face and figure, her smile and twinkling eyes, and her good-natured voice remained long with me as a pleasant memory."

Shortly after this intriguing vision, Elder Shreeve arrived in New Zealand to begin his missionary labors. He stated; "Before I had been a very long time in New Zealand, I saw her again; but this next time her presence was more than a fleeting fancy." Two months after his arrival in the country, a member of his branch asked Elder Shreeve to accompany him on a visit to an older woman, Sister Emmas, who had once been a member of the church.

Tom recalled, "I assented to his proposition and went to the house designated. When we entered we saw a little old woman sitting by the stove, smoking a pipe. She arose with some embarrassment at receiving visitors. But the moment she fully confronted me, I saw that she was the little old woman who had visited me in imagination on board the Wakatipu, and by comparison of dates I learned that on or about the very day when she appeared to me, she had been praying most earnestly that the Lord would bless her with a visit from a 'Mormon' Elder. She had often sat by her window and looked out with straining eyes and anxious heart for someone to come to her, and bring a renewal of the glad tidings which she had heard thirty years before in England."

Elder Shreeve became a frequent visitor and during their conversations, Sister Emmas told the missionary that she had often prayed to be visited by members of the church. She said she had a great desire to be united with her "people."

The elderly woman also told the young elder the circumstances surrounding her baptism. Sister Emmas said that she had been instantly converted as a young woman in England, after seeing two blind children receive their sight after being blessed by Mormon elders. However, her husband hated the Mormons and decided to move as far away from them as he could get. The couple settled in New Zealand, where for years Sister Emmas had yearned for contact from members of the church.

Now that she was happily reunited with the church, Sister Emmas was eager for Elder Shreeve to teach her more about the doctrine of the church, since she'd had so little opportunity to learn much about the gospel after her baptism. Tom adds, "While I remained in that region Sister Emmas was very kind to me. She frequently helped me with money, and I was always a welcome visitor at her house."[16]

"You Have Come Back As You Promised"

A widow diligently taught the gospel to her young son. However, when he grew up, the boy turned away from the church, refusing to believe any of the doctrine he had been taught for so many years. The distressed mother prayed diligently and earnestly that the Lord would enlighten his mind so that he might believe in God and come back to the church.

One day during a visit, he and his mother began discussing the purpose of life. The mother bore a strong testimony regarding the reality of life after death and tried earnestly to persuade him to accept the reality of God's existence. The son was unmoved by her declaration but thought of a plan that would placate his mother and effectively end their arguments about religion.

The disbelieving son asked his mother to make a promise, which was that if she died before he did, that she would return and let him know for certain if there was a life after this one. The mother agreed to this proposition, not knowing for certain whether she would be allowed to return.

In time, the mother did die and her son began to watch and wait for her return. Months passed and she did not show herself. Strangely enough, instead of increasing his certainty that there was no life after death, each day that passed without her appearance served to somehow multiply the uncertainties he had recently developed about his own views. Suddenly, he began to question his disbelief in God and was confused by the persistent and unusual feeling that his mother had taught him the truth. Even though she did not appear, the son began to feel more and more certain that his mother had been right all along. Finally, acquiescing to the deep feelings inside himself that had begun to blossom into a belief in God, he began praying that Heavenly Father would allow his mother to return and keep her promise.

Finally his prayers were answered. He was walking down the road when he saw a familiar-looking woman coming towards him. It was his mother.

The account states: "She looked natural as in life, and although the son knew she had been dead a long time he was in no way alarmed or frightened, and said, 'Well, mother, you have come back as you promised.'

"'Yes, my son,' she replied, 'but if you had known what trouble it has made me to get here, you would not have called me to come as you did.'"[17]

The mother was allowed to fulfill the promise she had made. Her appearance bolstered her son's faith and stood ever after as a testament to him that there was a God and that life after death was a reality.

Notes for Part Two

1 Heber J. Grant, *Conference Report,* October 1910, p. 119.
2 Joseph Smith, *Teachings of the Prophet Joseph Smith,* comp. Joseph Fielding Smith, (Salt Lake City: Deseret Book Co., 1976), p. 226.
3 Melvin J. Ballard, *Crusader for Righteousness,* (Salt Lake City: Bookcraft, 1966), p. 219.
4 A. Ad. Ramseyer, "Angel's Visits," *The Improvement Era,* vol. 20, November 1916, pp. 58-59.
5 Maha, "A Prophecy and Its Fulfillment," *The Juvenile Instructor,* vol. 25, 1 March 1890, p. 153.
6 *Ibid.*
7 *Ibid.*
8 Calvin Robert Stephens, *The Life and Contributions of Zebedee Coltrin,* (Salt Lake City: Church Historical Library, 1974), p. 7.
9 Andrew Jenson, *Latter-day Saint Biographical Encyclopedia,* vol. 1, (Salt Lake City: *The Deseret News,* 1901), p. 267.
10 Lloyd Milton Turnbow, *History of Zera Pulsipher,* (Salt Lake City: LDS Church Archives), p. 189.
11 *Ibid.,* pp. 189-90.
12 A.C. Nielson, *Latter-day Saints' Millennial Star,* vol. 58, 7 May, 1896, p. 301.

13 *Ibid.*, p. 302.
14 Augusta Joyce Crocheron, *Representative Women of Deseret,* (Salt Lake City: J.C. Graham & Company, 1884), p. 99.
15 *Ibid.*, pp. 100-101.
16 Tom Shreeve, *Helpful Visions, the Fourteenth Book of the Faith Promoting Series,* (Salt Lake City: Juvenile Instructor Office, 1887), pp. 62-63, 66-67.
17 Oliver B. Huntington, *The Young Woman's Journal,* vol. VI, January 1895, p. 189.

Part Three
Angels Comforting During Trials

Although the Holy Ghost is given to us as a comforter, Heavenly Father occasionally sends angels to provide additional support and consolation during our earthly trials. During general conference, Elder Jeffrey R. Holland spoke of how the Lord and His angels work to comfort mankind during times of trouble. "Christ and His angels and his prophets forever labor to buoy up our spirits, steady our nerves, calm our hearts, send us forth with renewed strength and resolute hope. They wish all to know that 'if God be for us, who can be against us?' (Romans 8:31) In the world we shall have tribulation, but we are to be of good cheer. Christ has overcome the world."[1]

God and His angels stay close at hand to support us during difficult moments. Heber C. Kimball declared, "He is near by, His angels are our associates, they are with us and round about us, and watch over us, and take care of us, and lead us, and guide us, and administer to our wants in their ministry and in their holy calling unto which they are appointed."[2]

Parley P. Pratt, an apostle who was himself comforted by angels, wrote about the wonder of being cared for by spiritual beings; "O, what a comfort it is, in this dreary world, to be loved and cared for by all-powerful, warm-hearted, and lovely friends!"[3]

Occasionally, as in many of the following experiences, the angels that are sent to earth to soothe and succor are departed family members. "O what an unspeakable blessing is the ministry of angels to mortal man!" exclaimed Parley P. Pratt. "What a pleasing thought, that many who minister to us and watch over us, are our near kindred—our fathers who have died and risen again in former ages, and who watch over their descendants with all the parental care and solicitude which characterize affectionate fathers and mothers on the earth."[4]

Departed relatives who serve as special ministering angels are often closer than we realize. President Joseph F. Smith pronounced, "I claim that we live in their presence, they see us, they are solicitous for our welfare, they love us now more than ever. For now they see the dangers that beset us; they can comprehend better than ever before, the weaknesses that are liable to mislead us into dark and forbidden paths. They see the temptations and the evils that beset us in life and the proneness of mortal beings to yield to temptations and to wrong doing; hence their solicitude for us and their love for us and their desire for our well being must be greater than that which we feel for ourselves."[5]

When God sends angels to provide relief from our hardships, we may be assured that such visits come because of the great love that Heavenly Father has for us. Heber J. Grant, in a message to the Church from the First Presidency, confirmed this, saying, "The Lord loves you. His angels are always near to help you."

"J Will Still Watch Over You"

On April 17, 1846, a small group of Saints left Nauvoo, intending to join the main body of Saints who were then at Winter Quarters. However, this band, which included Newel Knight, his wife Lydia and their seven children, faced many delays and by late fall, still had a long journey ahead of them. Because the imminent freezing temperatures and heavy snow would make it dangerous to travel, Brigham Young counseled the group not to continue but to seek out a good place nearby and remain there through the winter. When Indians offered the small group a place to stay, the Saints gratefully set up a temporary camp.

Then one night in January, 1847, Newel woke Lydia, complaining of an intense pain in his right side. She gave him a home remedy but his fever soared and the pain increased. Over the next few days, none of Lydia's remedies helped relieve his suffering and on January 11, it became apparent that Newel was dying. In agony, he spoke to his wife:

"'Lydia,' he whispered faintly. 'It is necessary for me to go. Joseph wants me. It is needful that a messenger be sent with the true condition of the Saints. Don't grieve too much, for you will be protected.'

"'Oh Newel, don't speak so,' Lydia replied. 'Don't give up; oh I could not bear it. Think of me, Newel, here in an Indian country alone, with my seven little children. No resting place for my feet, no one to counsel, to guide, or to protect me. I cannot let you go.'

"The dying man looked at her a moment, and then said with a peculiar look: 'I will not leave you now Lydia.' As the words left his lips, an agony of suffering seemed to seize him. His very frame trembled with the mighty throes of pain. The distracted wife bore his agony as long as she could, but at last, flinging herself on her knees, she cried to God to forgive her if she had asked amiss, and if it was really His will for her husband to die, that the pain might leave him and his spirit go in peace. The prayer was scarcely over 'ere a calm settled on the sufferer, and with one long loving look in the eyes of his beloved wife, the shadow lifted and the spirit fled."[6]

Lydia and her seven children were alone in Indian country. As they struggled with their grief, Lydia wondered how she could possibly take her family to Winter Quarters alone, and from there, undertake a journey of a thousand miles to reach the Salt Lake Valley without Newel to watch over and provide for them. To complicate matters further, Lydia discovered she was pregnant.

Three weeks later, Brigham Young received a revelation about how to organize the Saints so they could travel across the plains to a new home in the West. While most of the Saints rejoiced at this, Lydia felt nothing but despair. How could she prepare for a journey of a thousand miles without her husband?

Feeling lonely and discouraged, she found a secluded spot and, cried out, "'O Newel, why has thou left me?'"

The account states that, "As she spoke, he stood by her side, with a lovely smile on his face, and said: 'Be calm, let not sorrow overcome you. It was necessary that I should go. I was needed behind the vail to represent the true condition of this camp and people. You cannot fully comprehend it now; but the time will come when you shall know why I left you and our little ones. Therefore, dry up your tears. Be patient, I will go before you and protect you in your journeyings. And you and your little ones shall never perish for lack of food. Although the ravens of the valley should feed you and your little ones you shall not perish for the want of bread.'

"As he spoke the last words, she turned, and there appeared three ravens. Turning again to where her husband had stood, he was not."[7]

Lydia's spirit was revived and strengthened by Newel's consoling visit. Knowing that her husband was nearby, watching over her and the children comforted Lydia and gave her the courage she needed to face a difficult and uncertain future.

In April, Lydia left with the group of Saints for Winter Quarters. Her thirteen-year-old son, Samuel, drove one wagon pulled by oxen and James, who was nine, drove the other. After arriving at Winter Quarters, the camp split up. Those who were able to fit themselves up with new supplies, left for the Salt Lake Valley. Approximately ten families, including Lydia and her children, remained behind. Brigham Young directed them to make a temporary settlement about two miles from Winters Quarters, at a place called Ponca Camp.

That August, Lydia had a little boy. When the infant was only one week old, a sudden, violent rainstorm came up. Lydia lay in bed with her children gathered round her as rain began coming through the roof. She had her daughter Sally cover her and the newborn baby with all the bedding they had. When the top layers became soaked, she had Sally remove them. Finally, everything was completely wet and Lydia became chilled.

She told her daughter, "Sally, go to bed, it's no use doing any more unless some power beyond that which we possess is exercised, it is impossible for me to avoid catching cold. But we will trust in God, He has never failed to hear our prayers."[8]

That night Lydia asked God to watch over her and her children. Then her thoughts—as they often did—turned to her departed husband. She remembered how he always used to protect her. Shivering in the cold rain, Lydia cried out despondently, "Oh Newel, why could you not have stayed with and protected me through our journeyings?" Suddenly a beloved and familiar voice plainly answered her from out of the darkness.

"Lydia, be patient and fear not. I will still watch over you, and protect you in your present situation. You shall receive no harm. It was needful that I should go and you will understand why in due time."[9] When the voice ceased, a pleasant warmth crept over her, taking away the chill. Physically exhausted, yet inwardly at peace, Lydia drifted off to sleep. Although she woke in the morning still wet to the skin, she did not become ill.

Since Lydia did not have enough provisions to make the westward trek that year, Brigham Young told her to remain at Ponca Camp and asked if she would let other Saints borrow her oxen and wagons to make the journey. Lydia agreed. She stayed in Winter Quarters for several years but later, Lydia and her children made their way across the plains, arriving in the Salt Lake Valley in October of 1850.

"She Was Sent to Commune with Me"

Parley P. Pratt described his wife, Thankful, as tall and slender, having large dark eyes and black glossy hair. The couple longed for children, but Thankful had very poor health and was unable to conceive. However, after Heber C. Kimball gave her a priesthood blessing, she regained her health and became pregnant. Sadly though, Thankful died a few hours after giving birth to their first child—a son—born on March 25, 1837. Parley mourned his wife's death but was comforted to know that their love was eternal and that one day they would be reunited.

At this time, persecution against the Saints was steadily increasing. Often the leaders of the church found themselves cast into jail because of false accusations. Two years after Thankful's death, Parley was imprisoned on bogus charges in Richmond, Missouri, along with several other brethren. Days, then weeks passed, yet no progress was made toward achieving their release. Indeed, the jailers seemed content to keep them there indefinitely and regaled their captives with stories about how some prisoners had languished for years within those very cells. Parley began to wonder if that was to be his fate as weeks of imprisonment turned into months.

One day, the apostle became despondent when he appeared before a judge and learned that he and his brethren were no further toward being released than on the first day they had been jailed. Kneeling in the dark, cold and filthy dungeon, Parley began praying daily to know if he would ever be released to preach the gospel and be with his friends again. Finally, during one of those prayers, a sweet angel brought him a comforting answer.

He writes: "After some days of prayer and fasting and seeking the Lord on the subject, I one evening retired to my bed in my lonely chamber at an early hour, and while the other prisoners and the guard were chatting and beguiling the lonesome hours in the upper part of the prison, I lay in silence, seeking and expecting an answer to my prayer, when suddenly I seemed carried away in the spirit and no longer sensible to outward objects with which I was surrounded. A heaven of peace and calmness pervaded my bosom; a personage from the world of spirits stood before me with a smile of compassion in every look, and pity mingled with the tenderest love and sympathy in every expression of the countenance.

"A soft hand seemed placed within my own, and a glowing cheek was laid in tenderness and warmth upon mine. A well-known voice saluted me, which I readily recognized as that of the wife of my youth, who had then for nearly two years been sweetly sleeping where the wicked cease from troubling and the weary are at rest. I was made to realize that she was sent to commune with me, and to answer my question. Knowing this, I said to her, in a most earnest and inquiring tone: 'Shall I ever be at liberty again in this life, and enjoy the society of my family and the saints, and preach the gospel, as I have done?'

"She answered definitely and unhesitatingly: 'Yes!'

"I then recollected that I had agreed to be satisfied with the knowledge of that one fact, but now I wanted more. Said I: 'Can you tell me how, or by what means, or when, I shall escape?'

"She replied: 'That thing is not made known to me yet.'

"I instantly felt that I had gone beyond my agreement and my faith in asking this last question, and that I must be contented at present with the answer to the first. Her gentle spirit then saluted me and withdrew. I came to myself. The noise of the guards again grated on my ears, but heaven and hope were in my soul."[10]

The next morning, Parley related his experiences to his two fellow prisoners who were overjoyed to know that at some future time, they would be freed. Later, Parley remarked that to some people, seeing his wife might seem like an idle dream or the product of a wild imagination but that he personally regarded it as a reality. In time, Thankful's assurance that her husband would be free came true. With the help of fellow Saints on the outside who orchestrated a daring and sensational breakout, Parley and his brethren were able to escape.

A Voice Spoke Plainly to Her

Margaret McNeil Ballard was well-acquainted with poverty and sorrow. Although she had given birth to six children, two of them—twins—had died before they were a year old. During the next few years, Margaret gave birth to several premature babies who also died. Sickness further weakened Sister Ballard and when she became pregnant again, the life of her unborn baby was threatened. Margaret was confined to bed and prayed continually that God would spare the life of her baby.

One day, her husband took the children to see a parade. After they left, Sister Ballard dragged herself out of bed and trembling from weakness, knelt in prayer. She reminded the Lord of her willingness to obey the commandments and told Him that she had done all that was in her power to bring forth a new life. The ailing mother then asked the Lord for help in saving the life of her unborn baby. Her daughter, Myrtle, relates the marvelous experience that followed Sister Ballard's earnest petition.

"God hearkened unto her prayer, and a comfort was given to her. She saw no person, but a voice spoke plainly to her saying, 'Be of good cheer. Your life is acceptable, and you will bear a son who will become an apostle of the Lord, Jesus Christ.'"[11]

Margaret was greatly consoled by her heavenly visitor. As the angel prophesied, her son was born healthy. She named him Melvin Joseph and he did indeed become an apostle and served the Lord valiantly throughout his lifetime.

"Your Son Will Act as an Angel to You"

In 1839, Edward Hunter heard about a new religion, whose followers were nicknamed Mormons. He thought how strange it was that the general public seemed to detest them and yet no one could tell him the reason for their hatred. Edward's curiosity was further aroused when a member of the Church of Jesus Christ, Elder Davis, came to town and announced he would hold a meeting and share his beliefs. After overhearing some men making plans to attack the missionary when he spoke, Edward made up his mind to attend the meeting

On the appointed night, Edward watched and listened as Elder Davis spoke to the crowd and was insulted verbally and threatened physically on all sides. He felt a keen a sense of outrage at the extreme prejudice and intolerance shown against a young man who had done no harm and who was merely trying to explain his beliefs. Then Edward surprised everyone—including himself—by jumping up as boisterous men continued to disrupt the meeting by heckling the missionary. Edward called upon the audience to be fair and reasonable and allow the elder to speak his beliefs. Because of his strong show of support, the unruly men quieted down and did not carry out their threats.

That night at home, Edward was confused by his unusually strong, protective feelings toward a member of this unknown sect. Earnestly he prayed and asked the Lord, "Are those Mormons thy servants?"[12] Instantly a light, which was so bright that Edward had to shield his eyes with a blanket, appeared in the room. This heavenly sign was enough to convince him that Elder Davis had been preaching the true word of God. Not long after, Edward was baptized a member of the Church of Jesus Christ by Elder Orson Hyde.

A short time later, Hyrum Smith paid the new convert a visit. The discussion turned to the subject of the departed. Eager for information, Edward asked about his children who had died, being especially concerned about a little son named George, his most recent loss and a boy to whom he had been very devoted.

Hyrum replied, "It is pretty strong doctrine, but I believe I will tell it. Your son will act as an angel to you; not your guardian angel, but an auxiliary angel, to assist you in extreme trials." This prophecy was realized a year and a half later. At this time, Edward had become deeply depressed because of some unhappy circumstances in his life and was unable to shake off the dark and gloomy feelings that had become part of his day-to-day existence. Then one day, his little boy, George, appeared to him.

Edward states, "In appearance he was more perfect than in natural life—the same blue eyes, curly hair, fair complexion, and a most beautiful appearance. I felt disposed to keep him, and offered inducements for him to remain."[13]

Although it was not possible for the child to stay, Edward was greatly comforted by his son's visit. After telling his father that he had many friends in heaven, little George departed from view and returned to his heavenly home.

"From That Moment, I Had No More Fear"

Amanda Smith and her family stopped at Haun's Mill for a brief rest shortly before a vicious mob attacked the defenseless saints. During the assault, Amanda's husband and ten-year-old son were murdered and another young son was severely wounded. During that time of horror, Amanda was blessed several times with divine intervention. Once she received instruction on how to nurse her badly wounded son and another time, she received comfort and her fears were eased.

After the initial attack at Haun's Mill, it was feared that the mobbers might return to complete their deadly work and so, for the survivors, that night was one of continued panic. Outside her tent, Amanda could hear women and children sobbing and moaning with fear and grief over the loss of their husbands, fathers and brothers. Dogs howled in the dark over dead bodies while the bellows of terrified cattle rent the air. Amanda's stricken little boy lay before her, his grievous injury urgently needing the care of a doctor but there was none to be had. The little boy's wound was a ghastly sight for a mother to see. The entire hip joint had been shot away. Flesh and bone had disintegrated before the bullet, which had been fired at close range into the child's hip.

Amanda, not knowing what to do, cried out to God in anguish, "What shall I do? Thou knowest my inexperience. Thou seest my poor wounded boy, what shall I do? Heavenly Father, direct me!" Amanda's earnest prayers were answered and she heard a heavenly voice.

She states; "The voice told me to take those ashes (from an old campfire) and make a solution, then saturate a cloth with it and put it right into the wound. It was painful, but my little boy was too near dead to heed the pain much. Again and again I saturated the cloth and put it into the hole from which the hip joint had been plowed out, and each time mashed flesh and splinters of bone came away with the cloth, and the wound became white and clean. I had obeyed the voice that directed me, and having done this, prayed again to the Lord to be instructed further; and was answered as distinctly as though a physician had been standing by speaking to me."[14]

Amanda dressed the wound—which was so large it required a fourth yard of linen to cover it—with a poultice she was directed to make from the roots of a nearby slippery elm tree. She then moved her child into the nearest house she could find, a log structure that belonged to David Evans, a scant two miles from the scene of the massacre.

Since the mob had stolen their oxen, wagons and supplies, Amanda, along with a few other women and children, were unable to leave the area. For five trying weeks while her son lay on his stomach as he healed, Amanda and the others lived with the constant threat of being killed. Mobbers came frequently to demand the impossible—that the women leave immediately or face being exterminated, as their husbands had been. In terror and grief, the women turned to prayer for consolation.

Amanda says of that time; "In our utter desolation, what could we women do but pray? Prayer was our only source of comfort; our heavenly Father our only helper. None but he could save and deliver us. One day a mobber came from the mill with the captain's fiat: 'The captain says if you women don't stop your d—d praying he will send down a posse and kill every d—d one of you!' And he might as well have done it, as to stop us poor women praying in that hour of our great calamity. Our prayers were hushed in terror. We dared not let our voice be heard . . . but I could bear it no longer. I pined to hear once more my own voice in petition to my Heavenly Father.

"I stole down into a corn-field, and crawled into a 'stout' of corn.' It was as the temple of the Lord to me at the moment. I prayed aloud and most fervently. When I emerged from the corn, a voice spoke to me. It was a voice as plain as I ever heard one. It was no silent, strong impression of the spirit," she states firmly, "but a voice repeating a verse of the saints' hymn:

> That soul who on Jesus hath leaned for repose,
> I cannot, I will not desert to its foes;
> That soul, though all hell should endeavor to shake,
> I'll never, no never, no never forsake.

"From that moment, I had no more fear," Amanda stated. I felt that nothing could hurt me."[15]

The mobbers continued to harass the women and threaten them with death but Amanda had been strengthened by an angelic voice and was no longer in despair. After five weeks, Alma's hip miraculously healed, allowing the little boy to walk again. A flexible gristle had grown in place of the missing joint and socket—a phenomena that caused physicians to marvel. When her wounded son was well enough to travel, Amanda went boldly to the mobbers' camp and obtained a pair of steers, a horse and supplies. Thus outfitted, Amanda and her four surviving children quickly departed. Later they journeyed across the plains, arriving in the Salt Lake Valley in September of 1850.

"My Father and Mother Appeared to Me"

While returning home from a trip to Prescott, Arizona, in November of 1881, David Patten Kimball—the fourth son of President Heber C. Kimball—became lost in the Salt River Desert. After his rescue, David wrote about his harrowing experience to his sister, Helen Mar Whitney, and told her that during his ordeal, he had been visited by his departed parents. Following are excerpts from his letter.

"On the 4th of November, I took a very severe cold in a snow storm at Prescott, being clad in light clothing, which brought on pneumonia or lung fever. I resorted to Jamaica ginger and pepper tea to obtain relief and keep up my strength till I could reach home and receive proper care. On the 13th I camped in a canyon ten miles west of Prescott, my son Patten being with me. We had a team of eight horses and two wagons. That night I suffered more than death . . . On the 16th we drove to Black's ranch, twenty-eight miles nearer home, and were very comfortably located in Mr. Black's house.

"About 11 p.m., I awoke and to my surprise saw some six or eight men standing around my bed. I had no dread of them but felt that they were my friends . . . At this point I heard the most beautiful singing I ever listened to in all my life. These were the words, repeated three times by a choir: 'God bless Brother David Kimball.' I at once distinguished among them the voice of my second wife, Julia Merrill, who in life was a good singer. This, of course, astonished me. Just then my father commenced talking to me, the voice seeming to come from a long distance. He commenced by telling me of his associations with President Young, the Prophet Joseph, and others in the spirit world, then inquired about his children, and seemed to regret that his family were so scattered, and said there would be a great reformation in his family inside of two years. He also told me where I should live, also yourself and others, and a great many other things. I conversed freely with father, and my words were repeated three times by as many different persons, exactly as I spoke them, until they reached him, and then his words to me were handed down in a like manner.

"After all this I gave way to doubt, thinking it might be only a dream, and to convince myself that I was awake, I got up and walked out-doors into the open air. I returned and still the spirit of doubt was upon me. To test it further I asked my wife Julia to sing me a verse of one of her old songs. At that, the choir, which had continued singing, stopped and she sang the song through, every word being distinct and beautiful. The name of the song was, 'Does He Ever Think of Me.'

"My eyes were now turned toward the south, and there, as in a large parquette, I beheld hundreds, even thousands, of friends and relatives. I was then given the privilege of asking questions and did so. This lasted for some time, after which the singing commenced again, directly above me. I now wrapped myself in a pair of blankets and went out-doors, determined to see the singers, but could see nothing, though I could hear the voices just the same. I returned to my couch and the singing, which was all communicative and instructive, continued until the day dawned."[16]

That morning, David and Patten had breakfast with Mr. and Mrs. Black. As he and his son continued their journey, David pondered upon his father's words. Heber had reproved him for his sins and told him to repent. His father had also told his son that he could come to heaven right then, but when David expressed a desire to stay on earth a while longer, said that he could remain two more years.

At sundown, David and his son arrived at Wickenburg and had supper, taking a room at Peeples Hotel. On the 18th of November, they left Wickenburg, although David was feeling ill. His condition worsened as the day progressed. They camped out and that night he woke with a high fever, unable to think clearly. Confused and disoriented, he wandered out into the Salt River Desert. When David finally regained his senses, he was hopelessly lost. He wrote:

"When my mind was restored, and the fever which had raged within me had abated, I found myself lying on a bleak hill-top, lost in the desert, chilled, hungered, thirsty and feeble. I had scarcely any clothing on, was barefooted, and my body full of cactus from head to foot. My hands were a perfect mat of thorns and briars. This, with the knowledge that no one was near me, made me realize the awful condition I was in.

I could not walk . . . The wolves and ravens were hovering around me, anxiously awaiting my death. I had a long stick and I thought I would dig a deep hole and cover myself up the best I could, so the wolves would not devour my body until I could be found by my friends.

"On the night of the 21st, I could see a fire about twenty-five miles to the south, and felt satisfied that it was my friends coming after me. I knew the country where I was; I was about eight miles from houses where I could have got plenty of water and something to eat, but my strength was gone and my feet were so sore I could not stand up. Another long and dreary day passed, but I could see nothing but wolves and ravens and a barren desert covered with cactus, and had about made up my mind that the promise of two years life, made by my father, was not to be realized.

"While in this terrible plight, and when I had just about given up all hope, my father and mother appeared to me and gave me a drink of water and comforted me, telling me I would be found by my friends who were out searching for me, and that I should live two years longer as I had been promised. When night came I saw another fire a few hundred yards from me and could see my friends around it, but I was so hoarse I could not make them hear. By this time my body was almost lifeless and I could hardly move, but my mind was in a perfect condition and I could realize everything that happened around me.

"On the morning of the 23rd, at daylight, here they came, about twenty in all, two of my own sons, my nephew William, Bishop E. Pomeroy, John Lewis, John Blackburn, Wiley Jones and others, all friends and relatives from the Mesa, who had tracked me between seventy-five and one hundred miles. I shook hands with them, and they were all overjoyed to see me alive, although in such a pitiable plight. . . . They rolled me up in some blankets and put me on a buck-board and appointed John Lewis to look after me as doctor and nurse. After I had taken a few swallows of water, I was almost frantic for more, but they wisely refused to let me have it except in small doses every half hour.

"I had about seventy-five miles to ride home. We arrived at my place in Jonesville on the afternoon of the 24th of November, when my wife and family took charge of me and I was tenderly and carefully nourished . . ." David concluded his letter by saying, "Now, Sister Helen, during the last twelve years I have had doubts about the truth of 'Mormonism,' because I did not take a course to keep my testimony alive within me. And the letter I wrote you last August, and I suppose caused you to feel sorrowful, and you prayed for me and God heard your prayers. And our father and mother plead with the Lord in my behalf, to whom I will give the credit of this terrible but useful ordeal through which I have passed and only in part described, an ordeal which but few men have ever been able to endure and relate what I have seen and heard. . . I know these things were shown to me for my own good, and it was no dream but a glorious and awful reality . . . I know for myself that 'Mormonism' is true. With God's help, while I live, I shall strive to do good . . ."[17]

Although Indians in the area said that no human being could walk as far as David did, (the men that found him said he had walked between 75 to 100 miles) and go without water four days and five nights and remain alive, David survived his ordeal.

Two years later, almost to the very day after being lost in the desert and having his angel parents come and give him water, David passed away. His nephew, Charles S. Whitney, was with him and wrote the following to his relatives:

"Uncle David died this morning at half-past six, easily, and apparently without a bit of pain. Shortly before he died, he looked up and called, 'Father, father.' To-day is just two years from the day his father and mother came to him and gave him a drink of water, and told him that his friends would find him and he should live two years longer. He knew that he was going to die, and bade Aunt Caroline good-by day before yesterday."[18]

Notes for Part Three

1 Jeffrey R. Holland, "The Peaceable Things of the Kingdom," *The Ensign*, November 1996, p. 83.

2 Heber C. Kimball, *Journal of Discourses*, vol. 2, 17 September 1854, p. 222.

3 Parley P. Pratt, *Key to the Science of Theology*, 5th edition, (Salt Lake City: George Q. Cannon & Sons Co., 1891), p. 128.

4 Parley P. Pratt, *Key to the Science of Theology*, (London: Albert Carrington, 1877), p. 119.

5 Joseph F. Smith, *Conference Report*, April 1916, p. 3.

6 *Lydia Knight's History, The First Book of the Noble Women's Lives Series*, (Salt Lake City: Juvenile Instructor Office, 1883), pp. 69-70.

7 *Ibid.*, pp. 71-72.

8 *Ibid.*, pp. 74-75.

9 *Ibid.*, p. 75.

10 Edward Tullidge, *The Women of Mormondom*, (New York: 1877), pp. 227-29.

11 Bryant S. Hinckley, *Sermons and Missionary Services of Melvin Joseph Ballard*, (Salt Lake City: Deseret Book Company, 1949), p. 23.

12 Andrew Jenson, *Latter-day Saint Biographical Encyclopedia*, vol. 1, (Salt Lake City: *The Deseret News*, 1901), p. 229.

13 *Ibid.*, p. 230.

14 *Heroines of Mormondom, Second Book of Noble Women's Lives Series*, (Salt Lake City: Juvenile Instructor Office, 1884), p. 91.

15 Edward W. Tullidge, *The Women of Mormondom, op cit.*, pp. 129-30.

16 O.F. Whitney, *Helpful Visions, The 14th Book of the Faith-Promoting Series*, (Salt Lake City: Juvenile Instructor Office, 1887), pp. 10-11.

17 *Ibid.*, pp. 15-17.

18 *Ibid.*, p. 22.

Part Four
Angels Healing the Sick

God is mindful of our physical well being and watches over us tenderly. In Psalms we read; "He that dwelleth in the secret place of the most High shall abide under the shadow of the Almighty. For he shall give his angels charge over thee, to keep thee in all thy ways. They shall bear thee up in their hands, lest thou dash thy foot against a stone." (Psalms 91:1, 11, 12)

One of the early apostles of the church, Parley P. Pratt, explained the various duties that angels have in regard to our well being. He stated that an angel's business is ". . . to comfort and instruct individual members of the Church of the Saints; to heal them by the laying on of hands in the name of Jesus Christ, or to tell them what means to use in order to get well; to teach them good things . . . to warn them of approaching danger, or, to deliver them from prison, or from death."[1] We learn from this that occasionally God sends angels to heal people or to teach them how to overcome problems caused by their physical maladies.

When the gospel was restored, the holy priesthood was once again brought to earth. This divine power, given to man, can heal all those who are afflicted, as long as they have faith and when such healing is in accordance with God's plan. Heber J. Grant said, "I bear my witness to you that if a record had been made of all those who have been afflicted, those who have been given up to die, and who have been healed by the power of God, since the establishment of the Church of Christ in our day, it would make a book much larger than the New Testament. More miracles have been performed in The Church of Jesus Christ of Latter-day Saints than we have any account of in the days of the Savior and His apostles. Today, sickness is cured by spiritual power. In all humility, and with gratitude to God, my heavenly Father, I acknowledge freely and frankly that God saw fit to heal me, and I am a living monument of the healing power of Almighty God, which is in the Church of Christ."[2] The following stories relate touching examples of a compassionate and loving Heavenly Father sending angels to help ease the suffering of mortals.

"Thou Shalt Be Blessed"

Elizabeth Graham Macdonald was born in Perth, Scotland in 1831. In 1847, she learned about the restoration of the gospel and became convinced of the truthfulness of the Church of Jesus Christ. However, her family was so against Elizabeth being baptized that she had to leave home. The sixteen-year-old went to Edinburgh, where a member of the church was kind enough to take her in. Two years passed, then Elizabeth's father—who had become partially paralyzed during her absence—went to see her. Mr. Graham asked his daughter to return home, which she did. Elizabeth played a key role in converting her father and two weeks after her return, Mr. Graham was baptized and his paralysis left him.

In 1851, Elizabeth married Alexander Macdonald, who was also a member of the church. The couple wanted to have children, but Elizabeth was unable to conceive. As the years passed, she began to grieve about her inability to bear children. Then, in May of 1853, Elizabeth fell down a set of stairs and was seriously injured. Her recovery was slow and because she was confined to bed, Elizabeth had to be cared for by others.

One Saturday a neighbor, Mrs. Kent, came to spend the day. When she arrived, Elizabeth was feeling very depressed. To cheer her up, Mrs. Kent decided to go home and fetch a special treat, leaving Elizabeth momentarily by herself. However, Elizabeth soon discovered that she was not alone.

After repositioning herself in bed, Elizabeth said, "I was astonished to behold an aged man standing at the foot (of the bed). As I somewhat recovered from my natural timidity he came towards the head of the bed and laid his hands upon me, saying, 'I lay my hands upon thy head and bless thee in the name of the God of Abraham, Isaac and Jacob. The Lord hath seen the integrity of thine heart. In tears and sorrow thou hast bowed before the Lord, asking for children; this blessing is about to be granted unto thee. Thou shalt be blessed with children from this hour. Thou shalt be gathered to the valleys of the mountains, and there thou shalt see thy children raised as tender plants by thy side. Thy children and household shall call thee blessed. At present thy husband is better than many children. Be comforted. These blessings I seal upon thee, in the name of Jesus, Amen.' At this moment, Sister Kent came in and I saw no more of this personage. His presence was so impressed upon me that I can to this day minutely describe his clothing and countenance."[3]

Elizabeth recovered completely and early in 1854, she and her husband left Scotland and crossed the ocean to join the Saints. They arrived in Salt Lake City on the 30th of September. The angelic promise that she and Alexander would have children was fulfilled. Years later, Elizabeth wrote, "In 1872, my husband was appointed to settle in St. George, where we arrived about the middle of November. Here we have since remained, and I have taken great pleasure in this southern country, especially in having my family around me."[4]

Told She Would Live and Go To Zion

Maria Colebrook was born in 1848, in Chattenham, England. When she was a young girl, Maria attended the coronation of Queen Victoria, as did thousands of others. In the prodigious crush of people and traffic, her foot was accidentally run over and broken. The bones were not set properly and for the next eight years, Maria went about on crutches. Because her disability left her unable to play outdoors much, Maria turned to reading and spent much of her time pondering the scriptures. During her studies, one idea particularly interested her; that of a "wedding garment." While the current sectarian belief was that such clothing was meant figuratively, Maria felt that it was an actual garment.

Years later, Maria became seriously ill. She was recovering slowly when she had an extraordinary visit from twelve angels who were dressed in unusual clothing. The account states; "Twelve personages entered her room and passed around her bed, following one after another until her bed was surrounded. They each pointed to her as they walked, and the last one, who seemed to be the superior, stretched out his hand and laid it on her head. He told her among other things that they wore the wedding garment; that she should live and should go to 'Zion,' even though she did not understand exactly what the term 'Zion' meant. (They) told her what to use for her lame limb and how to use it. And while she gazed at them through the beautiful light that filled the room, they were gone. She was commanded not to tell all that was said to her, but that portion she did tell was considered a dream and accepted as a sure premonition of death."[5]

When Maria told her doctor about the instructions on how to heal her foot that she had received so miraculously, he completely disregarded the advice and insisted he needed to amputate. Maria refused to let him remove her crooked and afflicted foot, choosing instead to believe the promises given by the angels. The young woman was strict to do everything the personages had instructed. As Maria did what she had been told, her foot became more limber and she slowly regained her strength. In three months, she was able to walk.

Years passed and Maria grew up and married. A few months after the wedding, Maria's mother became upset about a beloved young friend's decision to be baptized into the Church of Jesus Christ. Her mother sent Maria to talk this mutual friend out of her plans to join the church and emigrate to Utah. Upon arriving at the woman's house, Maria disparaged her friend's desire to join the church, saying it was a useless sacrifice of her life and that her interest in the new religion was just a passing fancy. However, Maria's objections were cut short when she was suddenly overcome with severe spasms. She had suffered such cramps before but this time they did not abate after a few minutes as they normally did. Thoroughly alarmed, her friend asked permission to call the elders in to give her a blessing.

Maria scornfully refused, saying, "I would not permit such low creatures to touch me!"[6]

However, her condition continued to worsen. When it became critical, Maria finally consented to let the brethren administer to her. The elders arrived quickly and gave Maria a blessing. She was healed instantly. Such a remarkable recovery caused Maria to undergo a dramatic change of heart regarding the Church of Jesus Christ. Missionaries began teaching Maria and her husband the gospel and they were soon baptized. In 1850, Maria and her family left their homeland, boarded a ship called the Henry Ware, and emigrated to the United States, joining the Saints in Utah.

Although Maria was already convinced of the truth of the Church of Jesus Christ, her testimony was further strengthened when she saw the endowment robes used in the temple. It was exactly the same type of clothing—the "wedding garment"—worn by the twelve angels who had blessed her so many years before.

"A Glorious Light Came"

After their conversion and subsequent baptism, the family of William Wignell left Preston, England in May of 1856 to go to the United States. After their arrival, they made arrangements to go west and on August 27, left for the Salt Lake Valley. Unfortunately, during the journey, the Wignells' infant son became ill. His condition deteriorated until no one thought he could possibly survive. However, the infant was pulled back from the brink of death after being miraculously blessed by an angel. His father, William, wrote briefly about this experience.

"I wish to tell of manifestations of God to my wife. Our son, William H. Wignell was three weeks of age and was sickly and we had no hope of his recovery. An angel clothed in his endowment robes and appearing in a glorious light came and healed the boy and then disappeared. She can never forget it—the light was so beautiful."[7]

"All Pains Left Me"

Brother John J. was twenty-two years old when missionaries came to his parents' home in Sweden and taught him the gospel. He was baptized in 1857. Six months later, he became ill and was diagnosed with consumption. John continued to lose weight and his condition deteriorated. Eventually he became so weak that he was unable to eat and could only communicate by faint movements. His parents watched over him continually but had little hope for recovery. Finally it seemed that his last days on earth were at hand. About 10 p.m. one night, his mother—who was completely exhausted—went to bed, leaving him to his father's care.

John said, "The circulation of my blood ceased in my arms and legs, and I could only feel it slightly in my temples. About half-past ten I saw a man walk into the room through the door, but my father did not notice him. This person touched the top of my head with his fingers, and I felt a curious sensation, and the next moment I stood above my own body, that was lying motionless on the bed. As I looked around I saw the same mysterious person standing by my side. He was dressed like people are dressed nowadays, and I noticed that I—that is my spirit—also was dressed in that way, though I could not understand how this had happened, as I saw my body lying on the bed in my underclothes. This personage introduced himself to me as my guardian angel, and said that he was now ready to take me to my place."[8]

John was taken to a building where a great crowd of people were waiting for a meeting to begin. The angel and another personage went to the front of the group and spoke on the subject of repentance. When the meeting was over, the angels came back to John and the older personage told him that he ought to go back to earth. John replied that he was willing to go back, but that his lungs were very bad.

The man pointed at the other angel and said, "This one will look after that matter."

Then John stated, "My guardian angel led me back to my former bedroom, where I saw father still occupied in reading. I looked at the old clock on the wall and saw the hands pointed to 4 a.m. The angel again touched the top of my head, and I experienced the same sensation as when I left my body, but without any pain. The angel next took hold of my hands, and I felt as if an electric current passed through my fingers, hands, arms, and finally reached my lungs, and I could feel for half an hour how my lungs grew and expanded. All pains left me, and I spoke to my father, who had thought me dead all the time I had been away in the spirit world."[9]

"He Was All Dressed in White"

Called to be a missionary during a general conference session in 1875, Eli Peirce felt woefully unprepared to preach the gospel, since he had spent only a miniscule amount of time reading the scriptures during his life. Eli decided to remedy this situation by quitting his job so he could devote all of the time he had left before his departure to studying. Elder Peirce then traveled to Pennsylvania, where he was joined by Elder David Evans Jr. The two missionaries covered a 200-mile area, talking to people and preaching the gospel. During his ten-month mission, Eli was able to baptize fifty-six people.

Almost immediately after his return home, Eli was called to go on a second mission. It was while serving in Luzerne County, that he had an experience with an angel. It all began when Elder Peirce was asked to help administer to the youngest child of one of the branch presidents. Unfortunately, the wife of the branch president had become bitter toward the church and refused to allow any religious activity within the home. When the woman made it plain that she would not leave the baby's side, nor allow the brethren to bless her dying baby, the two men went upstairs to an upper room to pray for the infant. The mother, suspicious of their actions, sent one of her children upstairs to spy on them and report back.

Eli wrote; "In a secluded chamber we knelt down and prayed earnestly and fervently, until we felt that the child would live and knew that our prayers had been heard and answered. Turning round, we saw the little girl standing in the half open door gazing intently into the room, but not heeding our movements. She stood as if entranced for some seconds, her eyes fixed immovably upon a certain spot, and did not stir until her father spoke. She then said, 'Papa, who was that other man in there?'

"He replied, 'There was no other, darling, except Brother Peirce and myself; we were praying for baby.'

"She shook her head, and, with perfect composure, said, 'Oh, yes, there was; I saw him standing between you and Mr. Peirce, and he was all dressed in white.' This was repeated to the mother, who tried every means in her power to persuade the child that it was a mere delusion, but all to no purpose. Entreaties, bribes, threats and expostulations were alike unavailing. She knew what she had seen and nothing could shake that conviction."[10]

The child continued to steadfastly maintain that she had seen an angel and the faithful prayers of the elders were answered when the baby was restored to perfect health.

"You Shall Be Healed"

At first, Lorena Washburn Larsen was jubilant about being called to go on a six-month mission to the Manti temple as an ordinance worker.

But when Lorena was told she had to leave her children at home, she felt that such a separation would be almost more than she could endure. Lorena was obedient however, and after making arrangements for her children's care, left for Manti. After she had worked there for a short time, President Wells called her into his office. He told Lorena that she was needed more at home than at the temple and could return immediately. However, before she could make arrangements to return home, Lorena became ill. She sent a telegram to her husband and mother telling them of her illness. They arrived the next evening, the same night she had a visit from an angel.

Lorena recalled that evening, saying, "I lay praying that I might be healed. My eyes were closed, but I could see a man dressed in Temple clothes. He was standing by my bed. He said, 'You shall be healed, and go to the full time of your delivery, and bring forth a son, and shall call his name Enoch, for in him shall be a generation of usefulness.' When my husband came I told him about this experience, he smiled and said, 'It will be a great joke on you, if you have a girl.'"[11]

The angel's promise came true. Lorena was healed and carried the baby to full term. On August 22, 1889, Lorena had a son and named him Enoch.

"Three Personages Entered the Room"

When Wilford Woodruff received his patriarchal blessing under the hands of Joseph Smith, Sr., he was told that he would be delivered from his enemies by the mighty power of God and the administration of angels. Wilford testified, "This was marvelously fulfilled while in the city of London in 1840. Brothers Heber C. Kimball, Geo. A. Smith and I went to London together in the winter of 1840, being the first Elders who had attempted to established (sic) the gospel in that great and mighty city. As soon as we commenced we found the devil was manifest; the evil spirits gathered for our destruction, and at times they had great power. They would destroy all the Saints if they were not restrained by the power of God.

"Brother Smith and myself were together, and had retired to our rest, each occupying a cot, and but three feet apart. We had only just lain down, when it seemed as if a legion of devils made war upon us, to destroy us, and we were struggling for our lives in the midst of this warfare of evil spirits until we were nearly choked to death. I began to pray the best that I could in the midst of this struggle and asked the Father in the name of Jesus Christ to spare our lives. While thus praying three personages entered the room, clothed in white and encircled with light.

"They walked to our bedside, laid hands upon our heads and we were instantly delivered; and from that time forth we were no more troubled with evil spirits while in the city of London. As soon as they administered unto us they withdrew from the room, the lights withdrew with them and darkness returned."[12]

In another account of the same incident, Wilford added that he had actual wounds from his encounter with the evil spirits, but that his injuries were healed by angels. He states; "I fell asleep and slept until midnight, when I awoke and meditated upon the things of God until 3 o'clock in the morning; and, while forming a determination to warn the people in London and by the assistance and inspiration of God to overcome the power of darkness, a person appeared to me, whom I consider was the prince of darkness. He made war upon me, and attempted to take my life. As he was about to overcome me I prayed to the Father, in the name of Jesus Christ, for help. I then had power over him and he left me, though I was much wounded. Afterwards three persons dressed in white came to me and prayed with me, and I was healed immediately of all my wounds, and delivered of all my troubles."[13]

"It Was My Good Angel Watching Over Me"

Sarah Studevant Leavitt and her family were converted shortly after hearing missionaries testify about the newly restored gospel. However, Sarah, her husband and her daughter Louisa were not baptized until after they had made an 800-mile trip in the summer of 1835 and joined the Saints at Kirtland, Ohio. It was a difficult journey for Louisa, who had been sick for over a year and was still very feeble.

Most of the Saints who had traveled with them to Ohio moved on to Twelve Mile Grove in Illinois, but because her family was destitute, the Leavitts had to stay behind in Mayfield, a little village ten miles from Kirtland. Although Sarah and her family faced much persecution, they always tried to meet evil with good. Besides being troubled by the persecution, Sarah was worried about her daughter. Louisa remained in such poor health that she was confined to bed. One night, Sarah relates the following experience.

"I lay pondering on our situation . . . and prayed earnestly to the Lord to let us know what we should do. There was an angel stood by my bed to answer my prayer. He told me to call Louisa up and lay my hands upon her head in the name of Jesus Christ and administer to her and she should recover. I awakened my husband, who lay by my side, and told him to get up, make a fire, and get Louisa up. She would hear to him sooner than to me; to tell her that an angel had told me to lay my hands upon her head in the name of the Lord Jesus Christ and administer to her in His name and she should recover. . . she got up and I administered to her in faith, having the gift from the Lord. It was about midnight when this was done and she began to recover from that time and was soon up and about, and the honor, praise and glory be to God and the Lamb."[14]

Early in the spring, the Leavitts bought a farm in Five Mile Grove, which was closer to, but still seven miles away from the larger settlement. Shortly after their move in March, Sarah became ill with the chills and fever of malaria. When her condition worsened and she became confined to bed, a few women who lived nearby came by to nurse her. A dilemma developed when it came time for the women to return to their own families. They were afraid to leave Sarah unattended, fearful that the ill woman might die if she were left alone. They asked Sarah if she would live with them until she was better. When she agreed, they constructed a makeshift bed on top of an old sled to transport the ill woman over the prairie.

Sarah stayed with her neighbors for two months before she was well enough to even sit up. Finally, she returned home, although she was far from well and had to be nursed continually.

Sarah relates, "I had the chills while I lived at the Five Mile Grove and was reduced so low that the day I had the chill, after the fever was off they had to watch me night and day. If I slept over a few minutes I was overcome. Louisa and her father watched over me until they were tired out, as they had to work days. My husband said to Louisa: 'We must go to bed tonight. We can't be broke of rest so much.' I heard what was said and the first thought I had was it would kill me if I was not waked up. The next thought was that the angels will watch over me. I went to sleep and in the night some one touched me and waked me up.

I looked to see who it was that had waked me and I saw a person with his back towards me, going toward the fire. I thought it was my husband, but I felt unusual calmness and peace of mind. The next morning I found that no one had been up in the house . . . it was my good angel watching over me. The Lord fed me with a Shepherd's care. 'My noonday walk He will attend and all my midnight hours defend.'"[15]

"The Angel of the Lord Was There to Protect Us"

Elder H. Thorup was in Copenhagen in March of 1880, when he went to the small village of Salttofte. While there, he became acquainted with Sister Madsen and her daughter. Sister Madsen's husband was not a member of the church and was very bitter against it. He was a violent man and was often physically abusive to both his wife and daughter.

In March, Sister Madsen became very sick but did not dare to call upon the elders for a blessing, fearing that her husband would not allow it and might even physically harm either her or the elders. However, when Elder Thorup heard about her illness, he felt impressed to go and try to cheer and comfort Sister Madsen and her daughter. Mr. Madsen was not at home when he arrived, but was expected home at any minute.

He wrote; "Sister Madsen and her daughter were trembling with fear that he (Mr. Madsen) might come while I was at the house. But I felt that there was no power that could harm us, so I told the sisters to be of good cheer. After some conversation with the folks, Sister Madsen asked me if I would administer unto her, as she was very sick. I told her I would. I then took the consecrated oil and anointed her, then I laid my hands upon her head to seal the anointing, when I found that some unseen power had closed my mouth. After a few minutes had passed, a dark shadow was seen passing the window. As soon as that had left, my mouth was opened and I sealed the blessing of health, and commanded the evil ones to depart and not to molest this our sick sister. After a short stay I left them, asking God to be with them."

The next day, Elder Thorup happened to meet Mr. Madsen while walking along the road. Strangely enough, the man seemed very friendly and told him about the unusual experience he had the night before when he had arrived at his home. Mr. Madsen stated that he had discovered, before entering the house, that an elder from the Church of Jesus Christ was there and planned on administering to his sick wife. Mr. Madsen said that he was filled with anger and was just ready to throw open the door and storm inside to throw the elder out, but when he got to the door of the room where his wife was, he was stopped by an unseen power.

Then he heard a voice say, "Do not harm the man who is in thy house, nor thy family."

A strange feeling come over him and feeling powerless, he went back outside and passed by the window. It was Mr. Madsen's shadow that Elder Thorup had seen as he first tried to pronounce the blessing. The man admitted that he had hidden himself in a nearby shed until the elder had left. Mr. Madsen said that later, he felt a strange sense of gladness that he had left them alone.

Elder Thorup concluded his remarks by saying, "The angel of God was there to protect us, hence I felt safe to say to the folks that no power should molest us while I was at their house."[16]

Notes for Part Four

1 Parley P. Pratt, *Key to the Science of Theology* (London: Albert Carrington, 1877), p. 117.

2 Heber J. Grant, *Conference Report,* October 1910, p. 119.

3 Edward Tullidge, *The Women of Mormondom* (New York: 1877), pp. 458-59.

4 *Ibid.*

5 "Young Women's Journal," vol. 2, March 1891, p. 292.

6 *Ibid.* p. 293.

7 N.B. Lundwall, *Faith Like the Ancients,* vol. II (Mountain Valley Publishers: Manti, 1968), p. 23.

8 C.C.A. Christenson, *Latter-day Saints' Millennial Star,* vol. 55, 27 February 1893, p. 150.

9 *Ibid.,* pp. 150-51.

10 Eliza R. Snow Smith, *Biography and Family Record of Lorenzo Snow,* (Salt Lake City: Deseret News Company, 1884), p. 413.

11 *Autobiography of Lorena Eugenia Washburn Larsen,* (Salt Lake City: LDS Church Historical Library), p. 71.

12 Wilford Woodruff, *Leaves From My Journal, Third Book of the Faith Promoting Series,* (Salt Lake City: Juvenile Instructor Office, 1882), p. 95.

13 Matthias F. Cowley, *Wilford Woodruff* (Salt Lake City: Bookcraft, 1964), p. 130.

14 Sarah Studevant Leavitt, *History of Sarah Studevant Leavitt* (Salt Lake City: LDS Church Historical Library, unpublished manuscript, 1919), pp. 9-10.

15 *Ibid.,* pp. 17-18.

16 "The Angel of the Lord Was There," *The Juvenile Instructor,* vol. 30, 15 September 1895, pp. 670-71.

Part Five
Angels Consoling
When a Loved One Dies

One of the many reasons angels are sent to earth is to give special comfort to those who grieve after losing a loved one. Surely one of the noblest expressions of divine love is the interaction between heaven and earth when God bestows tangible assurance and spiritual sustenance in the form of an angelic presence when we mourn. The Lord has promised to support the faithful, saying, "I will be on your right hand and on your left, and my spirit shall be in your hearts, and mine angels round about you, to bear you up." (D&C 84:88)

Quite often, the angels who come briefly to earth in this capacity are departed family members who come to comfort the loved ones they have left behind. Elder Marion D. Hanks testified, "There are no casual angels who minister specifically to us. They are ancestors or loved ones who have gone on to heaven or they are spirits of posterity yet to come."[1]

President Joseph F. Smith also testified that when angels come to visit us, they are usually family and friends. "When messengers are sent to minister to the inhabitants of this earth, they are not strangers but from the ranks of our kindred, friends and fellow-beings and fellow servants. The ancient prophets who died were those who came to visit their fellow creatures upon the earth . . . In like manner our fathers and mothers, brothers, sisters and friends who have passed away from this earth, having been faithful, and worthy to enjoy these rights and privileges, may have a mission given them to visit their relatives and friends upon the earth again, bringing from the divine Presence messages of love, of warning, of reproof and instruction to those whom they had learned to love in the flesh."[2]

Loving relationships endure beyond this mortal life. Latter-day Saints know that families can be together forever when sealed by the power of the holy priesthood. This means that even though loved ones may precede us into heaven, we remain connected to one another and familial bonds will remain intact. It is consoling to know that even though we are not in the immediate presence of our departed loved ones, they still care about us and are concerned about our welfare. Because families remain linked, even though death temporarily separates individual members, it is not surprising that when God dispatches an angel to earth to comfort the bereaved, he often sends someone who is related to us. The following stories are a comforting witness that beloved angels are near and console us when we mourn.

"I Am Where Jesus Is"

Lydia and Hannah Cornaby were not only sisters but close friends as well. However, the two were separated on August 7, 1836, when Lydia, who was then only eleven, passed away. Hannah, who was fourteen years old at the time, was in despair. Time did not diminish her anguish and eventually, Hannah's fierce and unrelenting grief began to affect her physical well-being. Then, she had a remarkable experience.

She writes; "I mourned so deeply that my health became impaired ... Meanwhile, I was praying to God for help to control my grief, desiring again to see my beloved sister and this desire was granted me. One Sunday afternoon, feeling too unwell to go to church, I remained at home, the other members of the family attending. Thus alone, my thoughts reverted to my sister; and lo! She stood before me, as when in perfect health and loveliness. My first impulse was to embrace her, but she moved from me, saying, 'No dear, you cannot.' I was disappointed at this, and tried again to clasp her in my arms; but she again assured me I could not, and I had to be content to talk to her at a distance. I asked her if she lived in Heaven; she replied, 'I am where Jesus is, will that satisfy you?'

"I said, 'Yes,' and asked how her clothes had been kept so well.

"She replied, 'You remember, that while the children of Israel traveled in the wilderness, their clothes did not wax old; mine are preserved on the same principle.'

"After some further conversation, she disappeared, keeping her face towards me until she vanished from sight. During her stay and after she left I was not in the least alarmed. I knew she had come from the spirit world to gratify my longing desire to see her. On their return, I told my parents what had happened and they thought it was a dream but I knew I was awake at the time."[3]

"I Have Taken Them to Myself"

After Joseph and Hyrum Smith were murdered at Carthage jail, their bodies were taken home to be washed and dressed in burial clothes. When those tasks were completed, their mother, Lucy Smith, entered the room where her sons' bodies lay. Lucy was privileged to hear a voice comfort her, when she was feeling overwhelmed with grief.

Before entering the room where Joseph and Hyrum lay, Lucy admits, "I had for a long time braced every nerve, roused every energy of my soul, and called upon God to strengthen me; but when I entered the room, and saw my murdered sons extended both at once before my eyes, and heard the sobs and groans of my family, and the cries of 'Father! Husband! Brothers!' from the lips of their wives, children, brothers and sisters, it was too much, I sank back, crying to the Lord, in the agony of my soul, 'My God, my God, why hast thou forsaken this family!'

"A voice replied, 'I have taken them to myself, that they might have rest.' Emma was carried back to her room almost in a state of insensibility. Her oldest son approached the corpse, and dropped upon his knees, and laying his cheek against his father's, and kissing him, exclaimed, 'Oh, my father! My father!'

"As for myself, I was swallowed up in the depths of my afflictions; and though my soul was filled with horror past imagination, yet I was dumb, until I arose again to contemplate the spectacle before me. Oh! At that moment how my mind flew through every scene of sorrow and distress which we had passed, together, in which they had shown the innocence and sympathy which filled their guileless hearts. As I looked upon their peaceful, smiling countenances, I seemed almost to hear them say—'Mother, weep not for us, we have overcome the world by love; we carried to them the gospel, that their souls might be saved; they slew us for our testimony, and thus placed us beyond their power; their ascendancy is for a moment, ours is an eternal triumph.' I then thought upon the promise which I had received in Missouri, that in five years Joseph should have power over all his enemies. The time had elapsed and the promise was fulfilled."[4]

"I Dwell in a Beautiful Place"

While Lorenzo Snow was on a mission to Italy in 1850, one of his wives, Charlotte, died on September 25. Not long after, Lorenzo wrote in his journal about an extraordinary vision Sister Woodard had regarding his wife. He recorded; "A short time after Charlotte's decease, while I was in Italy, a sister in London, a very faithful Saint, the wife of Elder Jabez Woodard, had an open vision, in which she saw a beautiful woman, the most lovely being she ever beheld, clothed in white robes and crowned with glory. This personage told Mrs. Woodard that she was a wife of Lorenzo Snow."[5]

Sister Woodard was not the only one to see the departed Charlotte. Sarah Ann, another wife of Lorenzo Snow, had been living with Charlotte in a log house while Lorenzo was in Italy. After Charlotte died, Sarah Ann was so upset at her passing that she could not even think of sleeping in the room where Charlotte had died. At least, not until her sister-wife appeared to her. Sarah Ann related the angelic visit to Eliza R. Snow, who then wrote the following account.

"The family were all seated in their dining room, when a very bright light, above the brightness of the sun, burst into the apartment, and in the midst of that light Charlotte entered, sat down and took her little daughter, Roxey Charlotte on her lap, and the extra light in which she came disappeared. She said she was happy, which her calm, settled expression verified.

"She said, 'I dwell in a beautiful place.' The brilliant light returned after a short time, and Charlotte went as she came, in the midst of the light. At this time," Eliza relates, "Sarah Ann was fully awake, and although no moon was shining at the time, her room was sufficiently lighted that (as she describes it) 'one could see to pick up a pin.'"[6]

Seeing Charlotte so tranquil and happy alleviated much of Sarah Ann's distress and grief, enabling her to once again sleep in the bedroom she had once shared with Charlotte.

"Waiting for His Baby Brother"

In March of 1846, Joseph and Susannah Harker left Europe and came to America. Tragedy struck when their first-born son, John, drowned in the Mississippi River. After persecution forced them to leave Nauvoo, they traveled to Winter Quarters where they spent the bitterly cold winter near the river. Susannah suffered frequently from chills and fever and was very ill most of the time. Then, the Harkers' little one-year-old son, Joseph became ill. One night, when Susannah put him to bed, the baby appeared to be all right, but in the middle of the night he began to fuss and cry. Before his father could find the one candle which had been put away for emergency use, the baby was gone. Joseph and Susannah's grief was two-fold because it had only been six months earlier that their son John had died.

However, they were comforted by a marvelous visitation. The account briefly recounts Brother Harker's encounter with an angel. "Their grief at his passing was somewhat lessened because his father saw little John standing at the foot of their bed, waiting for his baby brother."[7]

"My Boy Had Gone Where He Was Needed"

Speaking at a funeral sermon, Heber J. Grant recalled that Wilford Woodruff had once said that he had set his heart upon his son, Brigham, who had died while still a young man. Heber said that he knew Brigham well and that Wilford's son was "one of the finest, brightest and choicest boys" he had ever known. He then went on to relate a few things that Wilford had told him regarding the loss of this son.

"Brother Woodruff said that all the days of his life he had acknowledged the hand of the Lord in everything which had come to him—life, death, joy, remorse, anything and everything—until he lost this boy. He said when his son Brigham drowned he felt almost rebellious about it. Finally the Lord was good enough to give to him a manifestation to the effect that he had a great work to do here—that is, Brother Woodruff—in the temples as soon as they were completed—and he did work in the temples with the assistance of his friends for thousands of his ancestors who had died without a knowledge of the Gospel.

"He was told by the Lord . . . that this boy of his was needed on the other side to carry the Gospel to his relatives for whom Brother Woodruff was to do the vicarious labor in the temples when they were completed. This reconciled Brother Woodruff to the inexplicable, though previously he could not feel satisfied regarding the loss of that boy. He said: 'I had lived in hopes that this boy would some day follow me. He was more brilliant than I am, and I hoped he might some day be one of the Apostles of the Lord Jesus Christ, and it was a terrible shock to me when he died. But I shall never cease to be grateful to the Lord for giving me a special manifestation to the effect that my boy had gone where he was needed more than he was needed here.'"[8]

"The Will of the Lord Be Done"

Lucy Stringham Grant had been very ill for many months. When there was no hope of recovery and her death was imminent, her husband, Heber J. Grant, called the family together to tell them the sad news. When Heber told the children that their mother was dying, one of his little daughters, Lucy, picked up a vial of consecrated oil and begged her father to administer to her mother once more. Heber was reluctant to do so, but because Lucy insisted, performed the ordinance. However, instead of praying for his wife's recovery, Heber dedicated her to the Lord. Lucy, having a keen mind at twelve years of age, understood immediately that her father had not administered to her mother in the way she wanted.

Lucy went immediately to her room and began praying that God would heal her mother. She was then blessed to have the following manifestation. Lucy reports; "As I was praying a voice said to me, 'In the death of your mother the will of the Lord will be done.' I was comforted from that moment and soon a beautiful spirit pervaded the house. A half hour later my mother passed away and then I told my father and other members of the family of the answer to my prayer."

Many years later, another incident in regards to the death of her mother was revealed. Lucy explains; "Years afterward at a meeting where my father was speaking I heard him tell this incident, and then add something that I had never before heard. He said: 'After I had anointed my wife for her death, I saw the effect it had upon my little girl and so I called upon the Lord and told Him that I was willing to acknowledge His hand in the death of my wife but I could not bear the thought that the faith of my little girl should be shaken in His Almighty Power. So I pleaded with the Lord to manifest to her that it was His will that her mother should go.'"[9]

A Visit from a Brother

Even as a young boy, John Taylor possessed an uncommon measure of the Holy Spirit. As a child, he frequently had spiritual experiences. He briefly stated, "Often when alone and sometimes in company, I heard sweet, soft, melodious music, as if performed by angelic or supernatural beings."[10]

Also, when he was a child, John saw an angel in the heavens, holding a trumpet to his mouth, sounding a message to the nations. No doubt this vision was symbolic of the restoration of the gospel. Perhaps it was even meant to indicate the instrumental part John Taylor was to play in spreading the news of the restored gospel when he became an adult. After his conversion to the Church of Jesus Christ, Elder Taylor went on numerous missions, taking the gospel to many nations and bringing countless new members into the church.

Later in his life, while speaking at a meeting, Elder John Taylor voiced the hope that God would enlighten him regarding his ancestors who had passed away without knowing the gospel. He then acknowledged that he had once had a visit from his departed brother, David John. Although his brother had been dead many years, Elder Taylor reported that he had enjoyed a long conversation with him.[11]

"Can't You See Her?"

Irene Condie was just a little girl when her mother, Elizabeth Condie, died. However, Irene was allowed to see her mother one more time. On May 7, 1889, Irene attended church on Sunday as usual. After the afternoon meeting, she and five of her friends, who ranged in age from six to thirteen years of age, decided to pick wild flowers and place them on graves at the cemetery. As the girls strolled along, picking flowers, they sang songs they had learned in church.

When the group reached the grave of Irene's mother, the girls became subdued. As Irene related how she used to comb her mother's hair and how much she missed her mother, tears began to fall. Finally, the girls turned to leave but they had only gone a short distance when they decided to return to the grave. All of them felt an intense desire to see Sister Condie. When they reached the gravesite, Martha Wainwright declared stoutly that she would not leave until they saw the mother of their friend. John Nicholson wrote an account of the incident.

"They began singing the well-known hymn entitled, 'The Resurrection Day.' When they reached the end of the first verse they seemed to hear a voice, which did not appear to be audible, say, 'That will do.' They all knelt down and prayed. I understood it to be a part of their petition to the Lord that they might see Sister Condie. While thus engaged they were all impressed to look upward. They did so, and beheld a strange sight. It was the form of a woman, clothes (sic) in white, with arms extended, descending rapidly to the earth. This personage came down close to the grave, but her feet did not touch the ground, being a few inches above it.

"The little girls were frightened at first and began weeping when suddenly Irene exclaimed, 'Why, it's ma.' The woman beamed upon them with a lovely smile, looked upon the flowers that had been placed on her grave and on the graves of her two children who had been buried near her remains, took off her head-covering and turned slightly around, as if to say, 'Do not be afraid; you see it is I.' She made no sound however.

"All the six little girls recognized the face and form as those of Sister Condie. Her hair naturally of dark color, was loose and flowing, and slightly mixed with grey, as Sister Condie's was at the time of her death. All fear left the hearts of the little girls and they were filled with joy and peace.

"Little Irene, addressing the personage, said, 'Ma, will you come home and have supper? Annie is cooking it.' The little group then left the cemetery and walked toward the house of Brother Condie, with what was believed to be the spirit of his wife Elizabeth, following a short distance behind, the girls going along a good deal of the time with their heads turned so as to see her. On getting close to the house all the girls rushed into the lot.

"Irene entered the house in great haste, exclaiming to her brother, 'Johnny, come along quick, and see mother. She is out here.'

"Johnny ran out, saying, 'Where is she?'

"'There she is, right there on that knoll, can't you see her?' Johnny declared his inability to see anybody at or near the place to which his attention was directed. The girls were greatly astonished at this. Brother Condie came out and he was in the same predicament as Johnny. He could not see anything, while the girls insisted that Sister Condie was still there. Finally the beautiful figure suddenly disappeared from the view of the girls also.

"Brother Condie exhibited to the girls, his deceased wife's portrait, and they all insisted that it was the likeness of the lady they saw. Their statement was written down and compared with accounts given by the girls separately to different individuals, and no discrepancy was discovered. I saw a written narrative of the incident six months since, and the foregoing are the facts as related to me one day last week by Brother Condie, and by his daughter Irene. I do not see any reason to disbelieve what is told by these innocent little girls. I have made a simple statement of the story, as I confess it interested me when I heard it. Perhaps it may interest others as well. Respectfully, John Nicholson."[12]

"Be of Good Courage"

After the martyrdom of Joseph Smith, Eliza R. Snow was blessed to receive a visit from the dead prophet to comfort her. The account states; "June 27, 1844, Sister Eliza was prostrated with grief, and besought the Lord with all the fervency of her soul to permit her to follow the Prophet at once, and not leave her in so dark and wicked a world. And so set was her mind on the matter, that she did not and could not cease that prayer of her heart until the Prophet came to her and told her that she must not continue to supplicate the Lord in that way, for her petition was not in accordance with his design concerning her.

"Joseph told her that his work upon earth was completed as far as the mortal tabernacle was concerned, but hers was not; the Lord desired her, and so did her husband, to live many years, and assist in carrying on the great Latter-day work which Joseph had been chosen to establish. That she must be of good courage and help to cheer, and lighten the burdens of others. And that she must turn her thoughts away from her own loneliness, and seek to console her people in their bereavement and sorrow."[13]

Eliza followed the advice of the prophet and just four days after the death of Joseph and his brother Hyrum, wrote a poem vividly describing the tragedy of the assassination. Eliza R. Snow continued through her lifetime to be a great leader in the church and wrote many poems and hymns that brought comfort and peace to church members.

"His Dead Wife Walked Into the Room"

George G. Bywater related the following incident, which occurred in Wales. "The wife of one of our brethren in a Welsh parish was nigh unto death with typhoid fever. Before she died, her husband begged her to come back to him from her heavenly home and tell him how things were there. She did so; one morning, a few weeks afterwards, the husband was sitting in his bedchamber when his dead wife walked naturally into the room. As she came towards him, his mind was filled with a hundred questions which he desired to ask; but she divining his thoughts, raised a restraining hand and said:

"'It is no use asking me those questions for I am not permitted to answer them. But I can tell you some things. We have our organizations and our meetings, just as you do here. We have our work and our duties to attend to just as you have on earth. We hold council meetings and talk over matters. At a council held recently it was decided to send for Brother _____ and Brother_____. In two weeks from today they will be called hence.'

"When the husband's heavenly visitor had departed he hurried to the president of the branch to tell him of the dream and to then warn the two brethren who were so shortly to die. But when he related his vision to the president, he was told to keep his vision quietly to himself. If the brethren spoken of were not to die, it would cause considerable talk and scandal, which would better be avoided under any circumstances. But in exactly two weeks from the day of the vision, the two brethren spoken of were blown up in a mine, and they were the only two injured."[14]

"I Saw the Spirit of the Little One"

In 1878, a prosperous businessman in Salt Lake City lost his firstborn child, a dearly beloved daughter. He was unable to reconcile himself to losing his little girl. In fact, her death nearly drove him out of his mind and his friends began to feel he was becoming demented. The grieving father became alarmed that this might indeed be the case, and even though he was not a member of the church, began to pray and fast. Each day when he was done with his work and night had fallen, he would go to a nearby orchard and kneel and prostrate himself on the ground. He sought the Lord humbly, crying bitterly and pleading for God to guide him.

Prompted by the spirit to work at increasing his faith, the business-man began reading the Bible and Book of Mormon. Prior to his daughter's death, he had tried to read the Book of Mormon but found it always caused him to fall asleep. However, he now declared that the Book of Mormon was the most interesting book he had ever read. Within six months, the man was baptized and shortly after, was called on a mission. He sold his business and traveled thousands of miles away to preach the gospel.

A month after his departure, his wife had another daughter. The new father did not get to know his little girl very well, for shortly after returning home from his mission, she became ill and died. However, on the day of the funeral, the father had a marvelous opportunity to see not only this recently departed daughter, but also the little girl he had lost so many years before.

He relates; "At her burial my wife and I rode in a carriage with the coffin between us. After lamentation by the mother over her child's fate . . . and my own vain effort to comfort and console her, my spiritual vision was opened by God's grace, and I saw the spirit of the little one whose corpse we were taking to the cemetery for the last earthly rite; and along with her, holding her hand and walking in a most beautiful place like a garden was the sister who died several years before. The two looked perfectly happy and contented, and both of them were running up to and taking hold of a woman's skirt like children in playful mood will do. The woman who, to all appearance was acting as mother or nurse, was a dearly beloved girl who died in her girlhood days in the old country, and never had been acquainted with these girls of mine in the flesh. But they apparently showed an acquaintance and knowledge of each other anterior to mortal life.

"To finish I may say that this girl, though dying in Europe long before these children were born in America, had been baptized for in the old endowment house, and had the ordinances performed for her in the St. George Temple by my wife; and as a consequence was the nearest according to relationship to look after the children on the other side of the grave. But the main point is that the children are taken care of and feel happy after death, though parents mourn and sigh."[15]

Notes for Part Five

1 Marion D. Hanks, as quoted by Elaine Cannon, in *The Truth About Angels*, (Salt Lake City: Bookcraft, 1996), p. 68.
2 Joseph F. Smith, *Journal of Discourses*, vol. 22, p. 351.
3 Hannah Cornaby, *Autobiography and Poems*, (Salt Lake City: J.C. Graham & Co., 1881), pp. 13-14.
4 Lucy M. Smith, *History of the Prophet Joseph Smith, by his Mother Lucy Smith*, (Salt Lake City: Improvement Era, 1902), pp. 277-78.
5 Eliza R. Snow Smith, *Biography and Family Record of Lorenzo Snow*, (Salt Lake City: Deseret News Company, 1884), p. 232.
6 *Ibid.*, p. 234.
7 *Joseph Harker Family History*, compiled by Hyrum Bennion, Jr. and Stella Richards, (Salt Lake City: LDS Church Archives, 1949), p. 32.
8 Heber J. Grant, "Comforting Manifestations," *The Improvement Era*, vol. 34, February 1931, p. 189.
9 Lucy Grant Cannon, "A Remarkable Experience," *The Young Woman's Journal*, vol. XXVIII, 1917, p. 111.
10 B.H. Roberts, *The Life of John Taylor* (Salt Lake City: George Q. Cannon & Sons Company, 1892), pp. 27-28.
11 *Latter-day Saints' Millennial Star*, vol. 50, 1888, p. 402.
12 John Nicholson, *The Young Woman's Journal*, vol. 2, 1890, pp. 66-68.
13 Andrew Jenson, *Latter-day Saint Biographical Encyclopedia*, vol. 1, (Salt Lake City: Andrew Jenson History Company, 1901), p. 695.
14 "Interesting Incidents," *The Young Woman's Journal*, vol. 9, 1998, pp. 503-504.
15 "Comfort in Bereavement," *Liahona, The Elders' Journal*, vol. 7, July 3, 1909, pp. 31-32.

Part Six
Angels Giving Guidance and Instruction

One of the most important reasons angels are sent to earth is to give direction and guidance to mortals. By allowing the spirit of God to guide us, we can make intelligent decisions that will prove beneficial for ourselves and our families. If we were left to ourselves and made important decisions drawn only on our own personal knowledge—which is often faulty and incomplete—we would make innumerable mistakes during our lifetime. By utilizing the help of angels that come to oversee, establish, and guide the affairs of men according to God's commands, we can receive blessed guidance.

President Brigham Young taught that angels are sent to act in God's name; to instruct and direct mortals. He said, "The Lord is not everywhere in person; but he has his agents speaking and acting for him. His angels, his messengers, his apostles and servants are appointed and authorized to act in his name. And his servants are authorized to counsel and dictate in the greatest and what might be deemed the most trifling matters, to instruct, direct and guide his Saints."[1]

Prophets have a special connection with heaven and all prophets—beginning with Adam and continuing on down to seers of the latter days—have had angels minister to them. Prophets serve as an intermediary between God and His people and God's word comes to us through the mouth of His chosen prophet.

Robert J. Matthews, dean of Religious Instruction at Brigham Young University, said, "The ancient prophets who were the leaders anciently are angels now, and a number of them have ministered to the earth in the latter days . . . all are engaged in the same holy work of the Lord . . ."[2] This statement has been verified by President John Taylor, who said that the Prophet Joseph Smith had been visited by many ancient prophets who returned to earth as ministering angels. President Taylor said, "If you were to ask Joseph what sort of a looking man Adam was, he would tell you at once; he would tell you his size and appearance and all about him. You might have asked him what sort of men Peter, James and John were, and he could have told you. Why? Because he had seen them."[3]

Many departed leaders of the church have—under God's direction—been sent to minister to leaders on earth. President Joseph F. Smith declared, "Joseph Smith, Hyrum Smith, Brigham Young, Heber C. Kimball, Jedediah M. Grant, David Patten, Joseph Smith, Sen., and all those noble men who took an active part in the establishment of this work, and who died true and faithful to their trust, have the right and privilege and possess the keys and power to minister to the people of God in the flesh who live now, as much so and on the same principle that the ancient servants of God had the right to return to the earth and minister to the Saints of God in their day."[4]

President Smith also said, "For I believe that those who have been chosen in this dispensation and in former dispensations, to lay the foundation of God's work in the midst of the children of men, for their salvation and exaltation, will not be deprived in the spirit world from looking down upon the results of their own labors . . . So I feel quite confident that the eye of Joseph, the prophet, and of the martyrs of this dispensation, and of Brigham, and John, and Wilford, and those faithful men who were associated with them in their ministry upon the earth, are carefully guarding the interests of the kingdom of God in which they labored and for which they strove during their mortal lives. I believe they are as deeply interested in our welfare today, if not with greater capacity, with far more interest, behind the veil, than they were in the flesh . . . I have a feeling in my heart that I stand in the presence not only of the Father and of the Son, but in the presence of those whom God commissioned, raised up, and inspired, to lay the foundations of the work in which we are engaged."[5]

The following stories are examples of how angels come to earth in order to guide and instruct not only church leaders, but ordinary people in their lives.

A Father's Instructions

Allen Huntington received wise counsel and a message from two special angels—his departed father and brother—in 1891. His uncle, Oliver B. Huntington, relates the experience that Allen had while hunting alone in the Henry Mountains.

Oliver reported that his nephew had "camped on a certain night at a spring of water, where there was good feed for his horse, which he hobbled or turned loose, I disremember which; but to secure himself from possible surprise by either white or red men, he went about two hundred yards distant and made his bed in a clump of brush, without fire. That night he was taken sick, very sick, with fever and was entirely prostrated by morning so that he could not get to the water."

Since Allen was alone in an isolated area, there was no prospect of receiving help. As time slowly passed, he began suffering greatly from thirst and his condition became critical. Finally, after many hours of suffering had passed, Allen had an extraordinary experience.

Oliver continues his narrative; "Suddenly there stood before him his father, Dimick Huntington and his brother Lot. Both of them had been dead many years. In relating this to me, he (Allen) said; 'Now, Uncle Oliver, some folks will say, Oh, he saw or thought he saw, but it was with eyes delirious with a fevered brain, but I know,' he continued, 'that I was no more delirious then, than I am now. Father and Lot stood there as real and as natural as they ever did in life.'"

The elder Huntington did not speak of his son's illness but was intent on giving him certain instructions to follow. Allen's father said, "When you get back home I want you to be re-baptized into the Church. Then I want you to labor among the Indians while you live. You need not work for the dead in the Temple, Aunt Zina and Uncle Oliver will attend to that." His father continued to detail certain duties he wanted his son to perform, being quite specific in his instructions. When the elder Huntington was done, he announced that he would be going.

Lot then spoke up, saying "Father, let us lay hands on Allen; I don't like to go away and leave him in this condition. They both laid hands on his head and pronounced a blessing for him to live and perform the work laid out for him to do. When that was done, Allen saw no more of them, but got up immediately, went to his horse and saddled him, and rode twenty miles that day."

Oliver stated that Allen carefully obeyed his father's instructions and concluded by saying, "I hope and expect that he will while he lives, continue to carry out his father's instruction, and if he does can promise that all will be well with him both here and hereafter."[6]

"One of the Most Wonderful Events of My Life"

After the Saints came west and were established in their new home in the Great Salt Lake Valley, the leaders of the church counseled the people to put their historical and genealogical records in order. Because of persecution suffered prior to crossing the plains, Solomon F. Kimball's father, Heber, had lost a portion of his journal but he still had a great desire to compile the remaining journals into a history of his life.[7] As a prominent church leader, Heber had little free time but as circumstances would permit, he worked with a friend to compile his history. Unfortunately, Heber died before his history could be completed.

In the fall of 1876, Solomon F. Kimball asked Edward W. Tullidge to finish his father's history and publish it. This was a laborious process, which consisted of wading through hundreds of blurred and dingy journals and packages of old, musty letters. Problems arose and work on the project was stopped. Nine years passed before Solomon felt impressed to finish his father's history. However, at that time he was unemployed and did not have the money to embark on such a huge project.

Then Solomon heard that the jailer had broken his arm. He hurried over to apply for the job and was promptly hired. Now that he had a small income, Solomon began receiving spiritual nudges from his father, encouraging him to finish the history. He states; "Soon after I had commenced work, it seemed to me at times as though I was in the very presence of my father. I could plainly feel his spirit working with me."[8]

Solomon talked with his family about finishing Heber's history and was able to gain the support of some members. Together, they decided to hire Bishop Orson F. Whitney to finish writing their father's history. The work went forward quickly. Then, on the day the history was to be bound into a book, Solomon had an extraordinary experience. He was giving the prisoners their breakfast when his father spoke to him.

Speaking of that day, Solomon declared; "One of the most wonderful events of my life took place . . . Imagine my joy and satisfaction when I heard the voice of my father's spirit saying to me that he had something more to go into the history, and would give it to me as a reward for my faithfulness in helping to bring that work forth. As soon as I could get the prisoners to work, I took a pencil and tab, and father's spirit told me what to write. Under his dictation I wrote for about twenty minutes. I scribbled as fast as I could, and a minute or two before I had finished, several prisoners who were doing janitor work came into the room, and father's spirit left.

"I undertook to complete the unfinished part but was unable to do so. Then I began to feel uneasy, fearing that Bishop Whitney would reject the communication. I went into the old Council Chamber and prayed to the Lord to prepare his mind to receive it. When he came to work that morning, I told him that I had just received a visit from father, and he had given me something more to go into the history. I handed him the communication. He read it over carefully and said, 'That is splendid.'"[9]

"Prepare to Receive the Word of the Lord"

The Lord often prepares people beforehand to receive truth and knowledge. "For behold, angels are declaring it unto many at this time in our land; and this is for the purpose of preparing the hearts of the children of men to receive his word at the time of his coming in his glory. And now we only wait to hear the joyful news declared unto us by the mouth of angels . . ." (Alma 13:24-25)

Elizabeth Ann Whitney and her husband, Newel K. Whitney heard angelic voices and saw a marvelous manifestation even before missionaries of the fledgling Church of Jesus Christ of Latter-day Saints came to their door. At the time, the Whitneys were associated with the Campbellites in Kirtland, but they were still seeking further light and knowledge.

Elizabeth Ann says, "We had been praying, to know from the Lord how we could obtain the gift of the Holy Ghost . . . We had been baptized for the remission of our sins, and believed in the laying on of hands and the gifts of the spirit. But there was no one with authority to confer the Holy Ghost upon us. We were seeking to know how to obtain the spirit and the gifts bestowed upon the ancient saints . . .

"One night—it was midnight—as my husband and I, in our house at Kirtland, were praying to the father to be shown the way, the spirit rested upon us and a cloud overshadowed the house. It was as though we were out of doors. The house passed away from our vision. We were not conscious of anything but the presence of the spirit and the cloud that was over us . . . A solemn awe pervaded us. We saw the cloud and we felt the spirit of the Lord. Then we heard a voice out of the cloud saying: 'Prepare to receive the word of the Lord, for it is coming!' At this we marveled greatly; but from that moment we knew that the word of the Lord was coming to Kirtland."[10]

Shortly after this spiritual manifestation, Parley P. Pratt, along with other Latter-day Saint elders, arrived in Kirtland and began spreading the news of the restored gospel. Elizabeth was baptized first and Newel was baptized a short time later in November of 1830.

"I Could Behold It With the Eyes of My Spirit"

Solomon Chamberlain had a female angel appear and give him a message—or rather a solemn warning—that was meant not only for him, but for her husband and many of her old friends. Solomon knew the angel—Sister Arnold—by name because they had both previously been members of the Quaker Society before converting to the Church of Jesus Christ.

Solomon relates the angelic appearance; "Here a circumstance took place which I feel it my duty to mention. One Monday morning while at work in my shop I was taken with a weakness through my whole system, the cause I could not tell, I was well in body but the exercise increased more and more, and in awful awe and glory . . . the presence of Christ filled the room, and my mind was wonderfully drawn up into heaven . . . My exercise increased till Wednesday in the after-noon. I was in a continual scene of prayer all this while. I now cried with a vocal voice and said Holy Ghost teach me from the eternal world, and I prayed in faith. That moment there was a departed spirit entered the room.

"The reader may wonder how I should know that there was a departed spirit in the room and could not behold it with my bodily eyes, but I could behold it with the eyes of my spirit; it was a woman that formerly had belonged to the society, (Quakers) and died happy in the Lord; she was the wife of Daniel Arnold, she saluted me with these words, 'don't you remember the exhortation that I gave you while on my dying bed.'

"I now knew her in a moment, and said 'yes, that I do sister spirit.' Now the exhortation was this, she exhorted me to live more obedient to God, and not live so light and trifling—be more sober and watchful . . . tell my husband he must repent and do his first works, or where I am he never can come. This man had backslided from God, in heart & had a name to live in the church. The spirit gave me a message for a number of the society of like cases, and gave me a charge to be faithful and go and deliver them at their meeting. Sunday—she said they all would be their (sic) and that I should have an opportunity, & speak in the power & authority of the holy Ghost."[11]

"Get Up and Go Baptize Larsen!"

In the New Testament, an angel woke Joseph, the future husband of Mary, and gave him instructions from God. "Then Joseph being raised from sleep did as the angel of the Lord had bidden him . . ." (Matthew 1:24) In a similar manner, Christoffer Jensen Kempe was woken by an angel and given specific instructions while he was serving as a missionary in Denmark.

The evening of October 31, 1862, was a stormy one and Elder Kempe was grateful to find shelter from the driving rain in a barn. It was there that Christoffer had an angelic visitation. The account says; "Some time after retiring to rest he was aroused by feeling a hand laid upon his shoulder and hearing a voice tell him to get up and go to Aalborg and baptize . . . (Niels) Larsen, whom he had seen at the Saints' meetings— that if he ever joined the church he would have to be baptized the next evening. Obedient to the voice of the spirit, he arose and set out afoot in the storm. He walked the entire distance (forty-two miles) and on his arrival in Aalborg, he called upon Niels at his lodgings and informed him that he had come to baptize him . . ."[12]

Niels was astonished to see the audacious missionary on his doorstep—unannounced and uninvited—wanting to baptize him. The surprised young man asked the missionary what had prompted him to come, as Niels was a practicing Lutheran and—although he had secretly been investigating the church for some time—had never told anyone he had been thinking about joining it. Elder Kempe told him that an angel had said that it was important that Niels be baptized the following night. This was the spiritual nudge that Niels needed to commit himself to baptism. Having attended many meetings and gained a testimony that the Church of Jesus Christ of Latter-day Saints was true, Niels decided to go ahead and have Elder Kempe baptize him.

It was only afterwards that Elder Kempe came to understand the angel's warning that if Niels was to be baptized, it had to be then or never. At that time, members of the local Lutheran church were upset at how many of their congregation were leaving and being baptized into the Church of Jesus Christ. To curtail the defections, a group of wealthy women were asked to plan and organize a club that would encourage members to stay in the Lutheran church.

One of the women just named to take part in this club was a rich woman who had befriended Niels, who was physically handicapped. Because of his severe handicaps, the only way Niels could earn a living was by sewing, a skill his mother had taught him during his childhood, when he had been bedridden for years. His rich benefactress procured much handwork for Niels and made sure that all her rich friends employed him. It was only through her patronage that he could survive on his own.

If Niels had waited to be baptized until after the club was officially organized and began its crusade, the woman who had befriended him would undoubtedly have brought great pressure on him not to join the church. Because Niels would have been unable to live independently without her support and also because he felt greatly indebted to her for the aid and kindness she had given him, Niels would have found it nearly impossible to go against her wishes. However, since he was baptized before the new club was organized, his patron was not unduly upset about Niel's conversion and did not withdraw her support.

Awakened by an Angel

After Elijah defeated the false prophets of Baal at Mount Carmel, he traveled for one day, then, becoming weary, fell asleep. "And as he lay and slept under a juniper tree, behold, then an angel touched him, and said unto him, arise and eat." (1 Kings 19:5) In the early days of the church, another angel came to earth to wake one of the Lord's latter-day apostles, Parley P. Pratt.

This story begins late in the spring of 1834, when Joseph Smith gathered approximately 200 men, along with teams, supplies and arms at Kirtland. He planned to march nearly one thousand miles to Missouri, carrying supplies to the beleaguered Saints there who were suffering greatly because of intense persecution. Joseph hoped that this march, called Zion's Camp, would induce the governor to call out a sufficient force to restore law, order and justice to the Saints in Missouri.

Since Parley P. Pratt was familiar with the route the men were taking through Ohio, Indiana, Illinois and Missouri—having traveled it several times as a missionary—he was told to travel ahead of the camp and recruit members for Zion's Camp. Joseph told Parley that doing this would add to their numbers, serving as a deterrent against those who might attack them and that it would also increase the impact their march might have on the governor.

Following the prophet's directives, Parley often traveled miles ahead of the camp, preaching and inviting men to join Zion's Camp. As a result, he spent very little time with the actual camp. Instead, he usually journeyed ahead of the main group in a light buggy, which he used to bring back new recruits who had agreed to join the march.

On May 27, Parley traveled all day and most of the evening in order to return to camp. He woke early the next morning and after a quick breakfast, changed horses and was soon on his way to recruit more men. However, near noon, Parley became so tired that he decided to stop and rest. He let his horse loose so it could forage on the grass. The ground was flat and level, with no home or cabins nearby.

In his journal, Parley noted; "I sank down overpowered with a deep sleep, and might have lain in a state of oblivion till the shades of night had gathered about me, so completely was I exhausted for want of sleep and rest; but I had only slept a moment, when a voice, more loud and shrill than I had ever heard before, fell on my ear, and thrilled through every part of my system. It said, 'Parley, it is time to be up and on your journey.' In a twinkling of an eye I was perfectly aroused. I sprang to my feet so suddenly that I could not at first recollect where I was, or what was before me to perform. I related the circumstance afterwards to brother Joseph Smith, and he bore testimony that it was the angel of the Lord who went before the camp, who found me overpowered with sleep, and thus awoke me."[13]

"I Have Come to Watch Over You"

President Wilford Woodruff was blessed many times to see angels and receive revelation. He states, "I have had the administration of angels in my day and time, though I never prayed for an angel. I have had, in several instances, the administration of holy angels . . . The Lord revealed to me by vision, by revelations, and by the Holy Spirit, many things that lay before me."[14]

In 1835, Jesse Nathaniel Smith recorded one of President Woodruff's experiences that he related in conference while in Tennessee. Jesse recorded it in his journal as follows:

"Once in A.O. Smoots mother's house an angel appeared to him (Wilford Woodruff) and showed him a panorama of future events. Also of seeing a vision of thousands of the Lamanites enter the temple by the door in the west end of the building previously unknown to him. They took charge of the temple and could do as much ordinance work in an hour as the other brethren could do in a day . . . "[15]

Wilford Woodruff spoke later about that angelic visit. He said, "A personage appeared to me and showed me the great scenes that should take place in the last days. One scene after another passed before me. I saw the sun darkened; I saw the moon become as blood; I saw the stars fall from heaven; I saw seven golden lamps set in the heavens, representing the various dispensations of God to man—a sign that would appear before the coming of Christ."[16]

After the prophet was killed at Carthage Jail, Wilford Woodruff received many angelic visits from Joseph Smith. In a discourse given at Weber Stake Conference, in Ogden in 1896, Wilford mentioned those visits, saying; "Joseph Smith visited me a great deal after his death, and taught me many important principles. The first time he visited me was while I was in a storm at sea. I was going on my last mission to preside in England. My companions were Brother Leonard W. Hardy, Brother Milton Holmes, Brother Dan Jones and another brother and my wife and two other women.

"We had been traveling three days and nights in a heavy gale and were being driven backwards. Finally I asked my companions to come into the cabin with me, and I told them to pray that the Lord would change the wind . . . We all offered the same prayer, both men and women; and when we got through we stepped onto the deck, and in less than a minute it was as though a man had taken a sword and cut that gale through, and you might have thrown a muslin handkerchief out and it would not have moved it.

"The night following this, Joseph and Hyrum visited me, and the Prophet laid before me a great many things. Among other things, he told me to get the Spirit of God; that all of us needed it. He also told me what the Twelve Apostles would be called to go through on the earth before the coming of the Son of Man, and what the reward of their labors would be . . .

"Joseph continued visiting myself and others up to a certain time, and then it stopped. The last time I saw him was in heaven. In the night vision I saw him at the door of the temple in heaven. He came and spoke to me. He said he could not stop to talk with me because he was in a hurry. I met a half dozen brethren who had held high positions on earth and none of them could stop to talk with me, because they were in a hurry. I was much astonished.

"By and by, I saw the Prophet again, and I got the privilege to ask him a question. 'Now,' said I, 'I want to know why you are in a hurry. I have been in a hurry all through my life, but I expected my hurry would be over when I got into the Kingdom of Heaven, if I ever did.'

"Joseph said, 'I will tell you, brother Woodruff; every dispensation that has had the priesthood on the earth and has gone into the celestial kingdom has had a certain amount of work to do to prepare to go to the earth with the Savior when he goes to reign on the earth. Each dispensation has had ample time to do this work. We have not. We are the last dispensation, and so much work has to be done and we need to be in a hurry in order to accomplish it.' Of course, that was satisfactory with me, but it was new doctrine to me."[17]

At general conference, Wilford Woodruff once again mentioned meeting with Joseph Smith and added that he had also seen many departed leaders of the church. He declared, "I believe the eyes of the heavenly hosts are over this people; I believe they are watching the elders of Israel, the prophets and apostles and men who are called to bear off this kingdom. I believe they watch over us all with great interest."

Wilford continued by saying that although he had many interviews with Brother Joseph, he had not seen the prophet during the last fifteen or twenty years. He added, "But during my travels in the southern country last winter, I had many interviews with President Young, and with Heber C. Kimball, and Geo. A. Smith, and Jedediah M. Grant, and many others who are dead. They attended our conference, they attended our meetings. And on one occasion, I saw Brother Brigham and Brother Heber ride in a carriage ahead of the carriage in which I rode when I was on my way to attend conference; and they were dressed in the most priestly robes. When we arrived at our destination, I asked Prest. (sic)Young if he would preach to us.

"He said, 'No, I have finished my testimony in the flesh I shall not talk to this people any more. But (said he) I have come to see you; I have come to watch over you, and to see what the people are doing. Then (said he) I want you to teach the people—and I want you to follow this counsel yourself—that they must labor and so live as to obtain the Holy Spirit, for without this you cannot build up the kingdom; without the spirit of God you are in danger of walking in the dark, and in danger of failing to accomplish your calling as apostles and as elders in the church and kingdom of God.'"

President Woodruff then pleaded with church members, exclaiming, "I do hope and pray God that we may magnify our priesthood and calling while we tarry here, so that when we get through our earthly mission and go into the spirit world, we may meet with Brothers Joseph and Brigham and Heber and the rest of the faithful men whom we knew and labored with while in the flesh, as well as Father Adam, Enoch, Abraham, Isaac and Jacob, and all the prophets and apostles who have had their day and their time and their generation and who have finished their work here below and gone home to glory. Do you not think they are interested about us? I tell you they are. And I desire when I die, and my spirit goes into the spirit world, to meet these men and to go where they are."[18]

"Be One and You Shall Have Enough"

Towards the end of the Saints' stay in Kirtland, persecution became extreme. Once, in order to save his life, Joseph Smith was carried away in a wooden box that had been nailed onto an ox sled. While most of the Saints made arrangements to leave the area as quickly as possible, there were five or six hundred people who were simply too poor to leave. Although their enemies threatened to kill them unless they left, the poverty-stricken Saints had no food, teams or wagons and were unable to comply with their demands.

Zera Pulsipher, a member of the First Presidency of the Seventies, along with four other members of the presidency, resolved to remain behind in Kirtland with the impoverished Saints until the means could be found to move them. The brethren held meetings to discuss how the people could be moved.

Zera states that after all their pondering on how to solve this dilemma, they "came to the conclusion we could not effect the purpose short of the marvelous power of God through the Priesthood. We went into the temple in the attic story to pray that our Father would open the way and give us means to gather with the Saints in Missouri which was nearly a thousand miles away." As they continued to ponder and pray for guidance, an angel appeared one day with heavenly counsel. Zera related that experience:

"One day while we were on our knees in prayer I saw a messenger, apparently like an old man with white hair down to his shoulders. He was a very large man, near seven feet high, wearing a white robe down to his ankles. He looked at me and turned his eyes on the others and then to me again and spoke saying, 'Be one and you shall have enough.'"

That succinct message was one all members of the presidency quickly understood, because it was a confirmation of an idea they had previously discussed, which was that they should pool all their means, efforts and property together into one fund, in order to move everyone.

Zera said that receiving angelic verification of their plan gave them great joy. He said, "We immediately advised the brethren to scatter and work for anything they could get that would be useful in moving to the new country."[19] That July, the group was able to leave Kirtland and begin the trek to Missouri.

An Angelic Warning

The Saints were facing great persecution in Nauvoo when an angel came to warn the Saints to flee. Although the people loved their city and had not yet finished the temple, severe persecution convinced many church leaders that it was necessary to leave. However, not everyone felt that a mass exodus was warranted. Almon W. Babbitt was among those who felt that the danger from the mobs had been largely exaggerated by church leaders. His business, as trustee of the church, was to dispose of property and he tried to coax people to remain in the city, feeling that having a large number of Saints in Nauvoo would afford them protection from the mobs.

On the other hand, Orson Hyde believed that a major bloodbath was a distinct possibility and had been asked to plan an orderly way for the people to leave the city. Yet much of his time was taken up simply in trying to convince people there was real danger in staying. He and other church leaders were continually frustrated at those who felt the peril from their enemies had been overstated and were only making lackadaisical efforts with their preparations to leave. Then, an angel appeared to Orson, declaring that time was running out. One of the first people Orson told about the angel's visit was Almon Babbitt.

The account states, "Orson Hyde told Babbitt that an angel had appeared to him to confirm that the complete exodus from Nauvoo was urgent."[20] This angelic warning helped put an end to the nonchalant attitude displayed by those who had been doubtful that leaving the city was necessary and doubtless saved lives and alleviated much suffering.

"This Is the Place"

One of the more well-known times when an angel has spoken to a prophet was when Brigham Young reached the Salt Lake Valley. Erastus Snow said that while crossing the plains in the late spring or early summer of 1847, Brigham Young beheld the Salt Lake Valley. The vision was so vivid that when Brigham saw the valley when coming out of the canyon, he knew without a doubt that it was the place that God had set aside for his people.

Elder Orson F. Whitney stated that although other men tried to persuade President Young to continue on and pass by the valley—which was then a forbidding, dry bit of desert—the prophet could not be dissuaded because of the vision he had seen and the angelic voice he heard when viewing the Salt Lake Valley.

Erastus Snow later said that when Brigham Young first beheld the valley, he "saw a tent settling down from heaven over this very spot, and heard a voice from above proclaiming: 'This is the place where my people Israel shall pitch their tents.'"[21]

Notes for Part Six

1 Brigham Young, *Journal of Discourses*, vol. 12, p. 245.

2 Robert J. Matthews, "The Fullness of Times," *The Ensign*, December 1989, p. 47.

3 John Taylor, *Journal of Discourses*, vol. 18, p. 326.

4 Joseph F. Smith, *Journal of Discourses*, vol. 22, pp. 351-52.

5 Joseph F. Smith, *Gospel Doctrine*, second edition, (Salt Lake City: *The Deseret News*, 1919), pp. 540-41.

6 Oliver B. Huntington, "Statement of Allen Huntington," in *Young Woman's Journal*, vol. 6, December 1894, pp. 129-30.

7 The lost journals are an account of Heber's second mission to England.

8 Solomon F. Kimball, "My Father Rewards Me," *Improvement Era*, vol. II, June 1908, p. 584.

9 *Ibid.*, p. 585.

10 Edward Tullidge, *The Women of Mormondom* (New York: 1877), pp. 41-42.

11 Solomon Chamberlin, unpublished manuscript, (Salt Lake City: LDS Church Archives), pp. 7-8.

12 George C. Lambert, *Treasures in Heaven, Fifteenth Book of the Faith Promoting Series*, (Salt Lake City, 1914), pp. 13-14.

13 Parley P. Pratt, *Autobiography of Parley Parker Pratt, One of the Twelve Apostles*, edited by Parley P. Pratt Jr., (New York: Russell Brothers, 1874), p. 123.

14 Wilford Woodruff, as quoted by Joseph Fielding Smith in *Answers to Gospel Questions*, vol. 2, (Salt Lake City: Deseret Book, 1958), p. 47.

15 Jesse Nathaniel Smith, *Journal of Jesse Nathaniel Smith, The Life Story of a Mormon Pioneer* (Salt Lake City: Jesse N. Smith Family Association, 1953), p. 393.

16 Wilford Woodruff, *Journal of Discourses,* vol. 22, 8 October 1881, pp. 332-33.

17 Wilford Woodruff, *Deseret Weekly News,* 53:21.

18 Wilford Woodruff, *Journal of Discourses,* vol. 21, pp. 317-18.

19 Lloyd Milton Turnbow, *History of Zera Pulsipher,* unpublished manuscript, (Salt Lake City: LDS Church Archives), pp. 191-92.

20 H. Dean Garrett, *Regional Studies in Latter-day Saint Church History—Illinois,* (Provo: Brigham Young University, 1995), p. 84.

21 Orson F. Whitney, *Conference Report,* April 9, 1916, p. 67.

Part Seven
Angels Were Among Them

In the past decade, people seem to have become uncommonly aware of angels. Part of the reason for this is because we are living in the final hours of earth's history. In these last days, angelic forces are coming to earth in greater numbers than ever before, to help mankind fight the forces of evil that are currently enveloping the earth in darkness. In response to the increasing wickedness of our day, Heavenly Father is sending heavenly armies of angels to our aid, so that we can stand firm in the battle against the incredible onslaught of wickedness that now defines our world.

Brigham Young declared that the war between good and evil began in earnest when the Prophet Joseph Smith received the golden plates. "When holy angels were sent from heaven to call and ordain Joseph Smith, and he to ordain others, the war commenced against sin and the power of it, and will continue until the earth shall be cleansed from it, and shall be made a fit habitation for Saints and angels."[1]

While we often hear about the armies that Satan directs to fight us, it is important to know that God has his own vast armies that are fighting for the right. Heber C. Kimball testified; "The Lord has hosts of angels who are qualified to defend us, and they have information enough to march armies and to select leaders to lead them against the enemy of the Saints; and the devil has leaders enough to march his armies against the Saints."[2]

Anyone who is striving to live in accordance with God's commandments has a right to the ministration of angels to help them withstand Satan and to help them in their lives. Jedediah M. Grant, second counselor to Brigham Young, said, "The Latter-day Saints try to live their religion, that they may converse with angels, receive the administration of holy messengers from the throne of God, be sanctified in their spirits, affections, and all their desires, that the Holy Ghost may rest upon them, and their hearts be filled therewith, and become competent to bear the presence of angels."[3]

As a general rule, people beholding spiritual personages have proven themselves faithful, although angels are sometimes sent to the wayward in order to call them to repentance. In the Book of Mormon, we read that angels minister according to God's command, "Showing themselves unto them of strong faith and a firm mind in every form of godliness." (Moroni 7:30)

Sometimes angels appear simply to make God's power manifest on earth. Other times, the motive behind their appearance is known only to God. But whatever the purpose, the appearance of an angel is not for the foolish, the over-imaginative or for people who have a doubting nature, for ". . . it is by faith that angels appear and minister unto men." (Moroni 7:37) Although there is usually an easily comprehensible reason for an angel's visit, the purpose may not always be clear and simple to understand, which is the case in many of the following experiences.

An Army in the Heavens

Vilate Kimball and her husband, Heber, along with others, witnessed an amazing battle scene in the heavens in 1827. Vilate recounts the episode:

"On the night of the 22nd of September, 1827, while living in the town of Mendon, after we retired to bed, John P. Green, who was then a traveling Reformed Methodist preacher, living within one hundred steps of our house, came and called my husband to come out and see the sight in the heavens. Heber awoke me, and Sister Fanny Young (sister of Brigham), who was living with us, and we all went out of doors. It was one of the most beautiful starlight nights, so clear we could see to pick up a pin.

"We looked to the eastern horizon, and beheld a white smoke arise towards the heavens. As it ascended, it formed into a belt, and made a noise like the rushing wind, and continued southwest, forming a regular bow, dipping in the western horizon. After the bow had formed, it began to widen out, growing transparent, of a bluish cast. It grew wide enough to contain twelve men abreast. In this bow, an army moved, commencing from the east and marching to the west. They continued moving until they reached the western horizon. They moved in platoons, and walked so close the rear ranks trod in the steps of their file leaders, until the whole bow was literally crowded with soldiers.

"We could distinctly see the muskets, bayonets and knapsacks of the men, who wore caps and feathers like those used by the American soldiers in the last war with Great Britain. We also saw their officers with their swords and equipage, and heard the clashing and jingling of their instruments of war, and could discern the form and features of the men. The most profound order existed throughout the entire army. When the foremost man stepped, every man stepped at the same time. We could hear their steps. When the front rank reached the western horizon, a battle ensued, as we could hear the report of the arms, and the rush. None can judge of our feelings as we beheld this army of spirits as plainly as ever armies of men were seen in the flesh. Every hair of our heads seemed alive. We gazed upon this scenery for hours, until it began to disappear."

Vilate added, "After we became acquainted with Mormonism, we learned that this took place the same evening that Joseph Smith received the records of the Book of Mormon from the angel Moroni, who had held those records in his possession. Father Young, and John P. Green's wife (Brigham's sister Rhoda), were also witnesses of this marvelous scene."[4]

Years later, after Heber and Vilate had joined the church, Heber asked Joseph Smith about the puzzling vision he and his wife had seen. The Prophet explained that it was symbolic of the final great struggle between the forces of good and evil brought about by the restoration of the gospel.

"The Room Was Filled With a Brilliant Light"

The Church of Jesus Christ of Latter-day Saints had not yet been restored to the earth when Daniel Tyler had a spiritual manifestation. Although he was not privileged to see the full form of an angel, he did see part of an angel's body. Daniel relates his encounter:

"About the year 1820, or early in 1821, I had a remarkable vision, which, after sixty-one years have passed away, is as vivid in my recollection as the scenes of yesterday. I had occasion to rise from my bed about midnight. Suddenly the room was filled with a brilliant light, brighter than the noon-day sun. I looked into the fire-place only to discern a few smouldering coals covered with ashes. I gazed upon everything visible in the house. All seemed natural except that the light gave things a brighter hue. I looked overhead to an opening between two loose boards or planks where my father usually kept his saw, auger and other small tools. There I beheld a hand and wrist which were nearly transparent, with a wrist-band whiter than the pure snow.

"I called to my mother, who awoke at the second call and inquired what I wanted. I asked who was in the chamber, and was told there was no one there, and that if there had been I could not have seen him in the darkness. I replied it was not dark. On my stating that it was lighter than day-light, and that I could see to pick up a pin, I was told to go to bed, which I did, when the vision closed, and it was so dark I could not see my hand before me, although I held it close to my face."[5]

Daniel's wonderful experience had a positive effect on his physical health. He had been suffering from a chronic ailment, but shortly after seeing the hand and arm of the angel, recovered completely.

An Angelic Prophecy

An angel told Orson Pratt about Heber C. Kimball's future role in the church shortly after Heber's baptism. Heber was introduced to the gospel in the fall of 1831 and was baptized early the following year. Not long after his baptism, Orson Pratt, a younger brother of Parley P. Pratt, stopped by for a visit. While Orson—a stalwart leader in the fledgling church—was talking with Heber, he heard an angelic voice prophesy about the recent convert. Elder Pratt said nothing about the voice at the time, but afterwards told Heber about his experience.

Heber later wrote, "While brother Pratt was talking with me, a voice spake to him and said, 'Orson, my son, that man will one day become one of my apostles.' I did not know this till afterwards."

Heber then stated that he himself also heard a voice, although it is unclear from his account whether it occurred that same day or at a later time. He said, "A voice also spoke to me and told me my lineage, and I told my wife Vilate that she was of the same lineage, and she believed it. I told her also that we would never be separated. I could tell you a thousand things that happened in that early day."

The prophecy that Orson Pratt heard came true when Heber C. Kimball was ordained an apostle in 1835. Ironically, that same year, Orson himself was ordained to the Quorum of the Twelve.

"It Was Prophesized That I Should See Joseph"

Mary Elizabeth Rollins Lightner was one of the earliest members of the church and well acquainted with Joseph Smith, his brother Hyrum and other church authorities. She was blessed to have several experiences with angels. One of them occurred when she went to the Lord in prayer, asking for guidance. Mary states:

"I went out and got between three haystacks where no one could see me. As I knelt down I thought, why not pray as Moses did? He prayed with his hands raised. When his hands were raised, Israel was victorious, but when they were not raised, the Philistines were victorious . . . I knelt down and if ever a poor mortal prayed, I did. A few nights after that an angel of the Lord came to me and if ever a thrill went through a mortal, it went through me. I gazed upon the clothes and figure but the eyes were like lightening [sic]. They pierced me from the crown of my head to the soles of my feet. I was frightened almost to death for a moment. I tried to waken my aunt, but I could not. The angel leaned over me and the light was very great, although it was night. When my aunt woke up she said she had seen a figure in white robes pass from our bed to my mother's bed and pass out of the window. Joseph came up the next Sabbath.

"He said, 'Have you had a witness yet?'

"'No.'

"'Well,' said he, 'the angel expressly told me you should have.'

"Said I, 'I have not had a witness, but I have seen something I have never seen before. I saw an angel and I was frightened almost to death. I did not speak.' He studied a while and put his elbows on his knees and his face in his hands.

"He looked up and said, 'How could you have been such a coward?'

"Said I, 'I was weak.'

"'Did you think to say, 'Father, help me?'

"'No.'

"'Well, if you had just said that, your mouth would have been opened for that was an angel of the living God. He came to you with more knowledge, intelligence, and light than I have ever dared to reveal.'

"I said, 'If that was an angel of light, why did he not speak to me?'

"'You covered your face and for this reason the angel was insulted.'

"Said I, 'Will it ever come again?'

"He thought a moment and then said, 'No, not the same one, but if you are faithful you shall see greater things than that.'"[6]

Joseph's promise was fulfilled when Mary was allowed to see the spirit personages of Joseph, Hyrum and Heber C. Kimball. She related the experience during a church meeting many years later, when she was very old.

Mary began; "I hope you will excuse me for being a little agitated but it is a terrible tax for me to come and get up to speak. But I want you to remember what I have said, that it is my testimony, as long as you live. I want to say to you as I said before that Joseph said if I was faithful, I should see greater things than the angel.

"Since then I have seen other persons, three came together and stood before me just as the sun went down—Joseph, Hyrum and Heber C. Kimball. It was prophesized [sic] that I should see Joseph before I died. Still, I was not thinking about that. I was thinking about a sermon I had heard. All at once I looked up and they stood before me. Joseph stood in the middle in a circle like the new moon and he stood with his arms over their shoulders. They bowed to me about a dozen times or more. I pinched myself to be sure I was awake, and I looked around the room to see where I had placed things. I thought I would shake hands with them. They saw my confusion and understood it and they laughed, and I thought Brother Kimball would almost kill himself laughing. I had no fear. As I went to shake hands with them, they bowed, smiled and began to fade. They went like the sun sinks behind a mountain or a cloud. It gave me more courage and hope than I ever had before."[7]

"The Walls Were No Bar Between Her and the Angel"

Elizabeth Comins Tyler had a remarkable vision shortly before the Prophet stopped by her home for a brief visit. She had not told anyone about the vision, except her husband, but when Joseph visited them on his way to Canada, Elizabeth confided in him. The Prophet assured her the vision was from God and startled Elizabeth when he told her that she had seen the same angel who had appeared many times to him. Elizabeth's son relates the incident as his mother told it to him:

"She saw a man sitting upon a white cloud, clothed in white from head to foot. He had on a peculiar cap; different from any she had ever seen, with a white robe, underclothing, and moccasins. It was revealed to her that this person was Michael, the archangel. She was sitting in the house drying peaches when she saw the heavenly vision, but the walls were no bar between her and the angel, who stood in the open space above her. The Prophet informed her that she had had a true vision, and it was of the Lord. He had seen the same angel several times. It was Michael, the Archangel, as revealed to her."[8]

"No Wings Were Visible"

Hannah Cornaby had always loved the Bible. Ever since she was a tiny child, her mother had taught her its precepts. Hannah memorized vast passages of the New Testament and Psalms and knew no greater joy than to read in the Bible. Because of her deep and abiding faith, Hannah rejoiced when—as a young girl—she saw an angel. In trying to relate the marvelous incident, Hannah said that no language could ever adequately describe it. Even after fifty years had passed, Hannah said a feeling of awe still came over her whenever she recalled seeing the heavenly being. She relates her experience as follows:

"My father and I were walking in our garden one evening, in the mellow twilight, and a quiet gray beauty pervaded the scene, when a sudden flash of light made us start; and turning toward the point whence it proceeded, we saw a remarkable streak of red, rising in the west, which captured our attention by its brightness. While watching its upward course, an arm, and a hand holding a roll were plainly visible; and soon the form of a person appeared, full in sight, following the streak of red before mentioned. A light, similar to the first, followed this wonderful personage, and the whole procession slowly moved through the midst of the heavens, then disappeared at the eastern boundary of the horizon.

"During the passage of this heavenly being across the entire arch of the sky, the right hand was in motion, waving the roll, as if showing it to the inhabitants of the earth. This wonderful vision having disappeared, my father and I, hand in hand, stood as if spellbound, when we heard two men passing along the road (from which a living fence of hedge separated us) discoursing on what they, as well as ourselves, had seen. The one remarked to the other that he thought it could not be an angel, as no wings were visible; we, too, had observed this, yet believed it to be an angel. A loose robe covered the body, leaving the arms and a portion of the limbs visible.

"As soon as we were able to walk, we went to the house. Mother saw that something unusual had happened and asked what made us so pale. At my request, Father allowed me to relate to her what we had seen. When I had given an account of this strange phenomenon, she was much affected and remarked that it was one of the signs of the last days, which, according to the Revelations of St. John, would transpire.

"I had loved God before; now I feared and reverenced him and desired to know more of that Being who rules in the heavens above and on the earth beneath. I loved to be alone, especially at eventide, to watch the heavens, thinking another angel would appear."[9]

"J Saw Two Jmmortal Beings"

Moroni 10:14 tells us that some people have the gift of "the beholding of angels and ministering spirits." This gift was given in unusual measure to a person known only by the initials, A.P. A firm believer in the Bible, A.P. states that after learning about the restoration of the gospel, he gained a testimony that Joseph Smith was a true prophet of God. Because of that testimony, when he became ill, he asked two elders to come and administer to him. In pronouncing the blessing, one of the elders declared that it would be A.P.'s peculiar privilege to enjoy the same gifts of conversing with angels that the prophet had enjoyed.

Thereafter, A.P. devoted every spare minute he could in prayer, reading the scriptures and pondering the principles of eternal life. Then, on the evening of February 21, 1867, after praying continuously for more than five hours, A.P. states that he had the grand privilege of conversing with angels. He recorded the following experience:

"The room was filled with consuming flames, as a rushing, mighty wind, and a pillar of fire far above the brightness of the noonday sun, shining with clear, transparent brilliancy, lit upon me, knocking me dumb and immovable, as it caught me up into a sitting posture. As I gazed mute and helpless toward heaven, in the midst of the light, just beneath the ceiling, I saw two immortal beings. Their countenances transcended the meridian sun, as stopping in their descent they smiled upon me. They then continued their dove like, gentle and circular descent, round and round, lower and lower, keeping an exact distance from each other—as we have seen swallows keep wonderful and exact proximity in following each other in their inimitable flights—till they had descended within a foot or two above me. They then rested their chins upon their right hands and smiled again.

"Oh! fallen, void and empty language, what word hast thou to describe the immortal beauty of an angel's smile? I now beheld the full and lightning like appearance of their countenances . . . They were dressed in robes of most exquisite whiteness and texture of pure linen, falling in gentle undulating folds to their ankles, which, with their feet were perfectly bare, as were also their hands and arms to the elbows. . . . One of them began speaking to me. But Oh! who can describe the voice? Softer than the echoes of a whisper, sweeter than undulating music and more refined than paradisiacal zephyrs, his words fell upon my adoring soul and dispelled every fear. 'Twas the voice of an Angel from Glory, never, never to be forgotten!'

"I then looked at the other angel and saw that it was a female. She spoke and told me her name. The first did not tell me his name, but spoke of the glory that I should enjoy after my afflictions in this world were over. Gazing at each of them alternately, I asked if they were married. The woman answered 'No. There is no marrying or giving in marriage in heaven, but it must be done on the earth.'

"When she had said this, I was dumb and could not endure their presence longer . . . The next change I remember, I was again gazing steadfastly at the two angels, from whose countenances I took not my eyes for a moment, and upon whom I could now look without pain or fear. As I was thus gazing and adoring them, desiring them to tarry and converse, I saw that the light was centering immediately around their persons then I knew intuitively they were going to leave me. And as I now gazed steadfastly . . . with the velocity of lightning a cloud overshadowed them that I could not behold them, though they moved not to the right nor to the left . . . I lay as one dead, without the power to stir a muscle or move a limb for about three hours.

"By day light I was able to get up and dress myself, but . . . felt so light in body for a week after, that I was half unconscious whether or not my feet touched the earth in walking . . . All glory and honor and blessing and power and might be unto the Father, and to His holy child Jesus, and the Holy Ghost, who are one God, for ever and ever worlds without end. Amen. (signed) A.P."[10]

"There Are Angels in This Room"

In 1899, David O. McKay was on his first mission when he attended a priesthood meeting in Glasgow, Scotland, where angels were present. He states, "I remember as if it were but yesterday, the intensity of the inspiration of that occasion. Everybody felt the rich outpouring of the Spirit of the Lord.

"During the progress of the meeting, an elder on his own initiative arose and said, 'Brethren, there are angels in this room.' Strange as it may seem, the announcement was not startling; indeed, it seemed wholly proper; though it had not occurred to me there were divine beings present. I only know that I was overflowing with gratitude for the presence of the Holy Spirit.

"I was profoundly impressed, however, when President James L. McMurrin (representing the European Mission presidency) arose and confirmed that statement by pointing to one brother sitting just in front of me and saying, 'Yes, brethren, there are angels in this room, and one of them is the guardian angel of that young man sitting there,' and he designated one who today is a patriarch of the Church.

"Pointing to another elder, he said, 'And one is the guardian angel of that young man there,' and he singled out one whom I had known from childhood. Tears were rolling down the cheeks of both of these missionaries, not in sorrow or grief, but as an expression of the overflowing Spirit; indeed, we were all weeping."

Then President McMurrin made a prophetic statement to young Elder McKay. He said, "'Let me say to you, Brother David, Satan hath desired you that he may sift you as wheat, but God is mindful of you.' Then he added, 'If you will keep the faith, you will yet sit in the leading councils of the Church.'"[11]

"J Want to Jnquire into Your Circumstances"

Bishop Roskelley, of Smithfield, Utah had a very unusual experience with an angel, which was related on October 8, 1881, by President Wilford Woodruff. The account states:

"On one occasion he (Bishop Roskelley) was suddenly taken very sick—near to death's door. While he lay in this condition, President Peter Maughan, who was dead, came to him and said: 'Brother Roskelley, we held a council on the other side of the vail. I have had a great deal to do, and I have the privilege of coming here to appoint one man to come and help. I have had three names given to me in council, and you are one of them. I want to inquire into your circumstances.'"

When Bishop Roskelley told the angel his current situation, President Maughan replied, "'I think I will not call you. I think you are wanted here more than perhaps one of the others.'"

Bishop Roskelley then began to recover from his illness. Shortly after, one of the men that President Maughan had mentioned suddenly became ill, but recovered as quickly as he had fallen sick.

He then asked to meet with Bishop Roskelley and confided, "'Brother Maughan came to me the other night and told me he was sent to call one man from the ward.' He told the Bishop that President Maughan had mentioned three names. One was his own, one was Bishop Roskelley and the third was another man in the ward. A few days after, the third man mentioned by the angel suddenly became very ill and died."[12]

Notes for Part Seven

1 Brigham Young, *Journal of Discourses,* vol. 2, 11 December 1864, p. 14.

2 Heber C. Kimball, *Journal of Discourses,* vol. 3, 2 March 1856, p. 230.

3 Jedediah M. Grant, *Journal of Discourses,* vol. 2, p. 279.

4 Edward Tullidge, *The Women of Mormondom* (New York: 1877), pp. 107-108.

5 Daniel Tyler, *Scraps of Biography, Tenth Book of the Faith Promoting Series* (Salt Lake City: Juvenile Instructor Office, 1883), p. 21.

6 Mary Elizabeth Rollins Lightner, unpublished manuscript (Salt Lake City: LDS Church History Archives), pp. 5-6.

7 *Ibid.,* p. 8.

8 Daniel Tyler, "Recollections of the Prophet Joseph Smith," *Juvenile Instructor,* vol. 27, 1 February 1892, p. 93.

9 Hannah Cornaby, *Autobiography and Poems,* (Salt Lake City: J.C. Graham & Co., 1881), pp. 9-12.

10 A.P. "A Vision," *Woman's Exponent* vol. 3, 15 February 1875, p. 139.

11 David O. McKay, *Conference Report,* October 1968, p. 86.

12 Wilford Woodruff, *Journal of Discourses,* vol. 22, 8 October 1881, p. 334.

Part Eight
Angels Helping People Leave Mortality

One of the times that angels appear most frequently is when a person has finished his or her mortal mission and is ready to leave this earthly life. Quite often, during this momentous occasion, the dying are met on the threshold of heaven by helpful angels who give them a loving welcome and serve as an escort during this transition.

Scholar and apostle John A. Widtsoe declared, "The main service of angels on earth is clearly to be helpers to humankind. They are watchmen, protecting and ministering to us in hours of need." (as quoted by Steven Osborne in, *Looking for Angels,* p. 31) Because one of the hours when we are in the greatest need is when we die, we can be assured that angels come to support and comfort us during the passage between mortality and the spirit world. Having an angel present at this time—to reassure and guide the dying—alleviates the concerns, worries and fears a person might have about leaving this life.

An additional comfort is given to the dying who have a testimony of God. ". . . it shall come to pass that those that die in me shall not taste of death, for it shall be sweet unto them." (D&C 42:46)

Once again, we find that many times the angels who serve mortals in this particular capacity are loved relatives who have previously died. Their function is to help ease the dying person's anxieties and to act as a guide to lead the person back to his or her heavenly home. While some loved ones who gather round the bedside may dismiss the exclamations of a dying person who appears to see and talk with long-dead relatives as the product of a weakened mind, those who believe in an after-life realize it makes perfect sense that departed loved ones would return to welcome them home.

Angelic visitations at the time of death provide solace to surviving family members and friends who witness those special interactions. The presence of spiritual personages, even though they remain unseen, touches the heart and mind of all present and increases the faith and testimonies of those left behind. The touch of heaven that angels bring with them when they come to earth often causes a surge of deep, warm feelings, a sensation Joseph F. Smith once mentioned when talking in the tabernacle.

Speaking frankly, President Smith said, "I hope you will forgive me for my emotion. You would have peculiar emotions, would you not, if you felt that you stood in the presence of your Father, in the very presence of Almighty God, in the very presence of the Son of God and of holy angels?"[1]

For an angel to appear at a time when mortals may be feeling understandably apprehensive, underscores God's tremendous love for us. In nothing are we left alone, not even in death, as the following experiences demonstrate.

"I Have Done and Suffered Enough"

Catherine Spencer was the youngest daughter of an affluent family and completely unused to the insufficient food and shelter that came as a result of severe persecution to the religion she had recently joined. As new members of the Church of Jesus Christ of Latter-day Saints, Catherine and her husband, along with their six children—all under the age of thirteen—were forced to leave Illinois and flee into the wilderness. Even though she was without adequate food, shelter and warmth, this stouthearted mother tried to cheer her family by singing as they traveled along. However, physical hardships took their toll on her health and Catherine became ill. Her friends wanted the sick woman to ask her family, who were not members of the church, once again for help. Catherine rejected the idea, since her parents had already refused to help her in any way because of her religious beliefs.

She replied, "No, if they will withhold from me the supplies they readily granted to my other sisters and brothers, because I adhere to the Saints, let them. I would rather abide with the Church, in poverty even in the wilderness, without their aid, than go to my unbelieving father's house, and have all that he possesses."[2]

Although Brother Spencer struggled to keep the rain and cold from his wife in their miserable circumstances, he was unable to keep her warm and dry. With continued exposure to the elements and a constitution that was already fragile, Catherine's condition rapidly deteriorated. Finally, believing that she would not survive, the feeble mother began instructing her children how to live and conduct themselves once she was gone.

With all the love of a mother's heart, she whispered to her offspring, "Oh, you dear little children, how I do hope you may fall into kind hands when I am gone!"

The account continues; "A night or two before she died, she said to her husband, with unwonted animation, 'A heavenly messenger has appeared to me to-night, and told me that I had done and suffered enough, and that he had now come to convey me to a mansion of gold.' Soon after, she said she wished her husband to call the children and other friends to her bedside, that she might give them a parting kiss; which being done, she said to her companion, 'I love you more than ever, but you must let me go. I only want to live for your sake, and that of our children.' When asked if she had anything to say to her father's family, she replied emphatically, 'Charge them to obey the gospel.'"[3]

The rain that had poured down so incessantly continued to do so and it was impossible to keep Catherine's bedding dry. Finally, in her last hours, Catherine mentioned her desire to be in a house. A friend was sent to a man named Barnes who lived near the camp to ask if they might bring the dying woman out of the cold and rain. He consented and Catherine was taken to his house. Soon after, she died. It appears that she found peace in leaving the trials of earth behind, for afterwards, a member of the High Council who was her friend, said of Catherine, "I never saw a countenance more inexpressibly serene and heavenly, than hers."[4]

"The Room Is Full of Angels"

When the Saints first arrived in Nauvoo, they found it full of swampy bogs and ponds with open, standing water, which made ideal breeding grounds for mosquitoes. Swarms of the pesky insects quickly spread the fearful illness of malaria, although it was not known at the time that mosquitoes were the carriers of that disease. The Saints called the sickness, which caused terrible chills and fever, the ague, and believed that it came from the musty, foul-smelling air caused by the rotting vegetation common to swamps and marshes.

When the Saints moved to the area, it didn't take long for people to become ill. At one time, there were fifty deaths within just a few weeks. One of those who fell ill was Colonel Seymour Brunson, one of the first elders in the church. Although his friends and family worked hard to save him, Seymour died at the age of forty. However, his passing was made easier because of a visit from a friend and the presence of angels who came to escort him home.

The prophet Joseph Smith came to visit Seymour as he lay dying. Apparently Joseph was loath to lose such a stalwart man, for it was recorded that, "A short time before he (Seymour) died, he told Joseph not to hold him any longer, 'for I have seen David Patten (an apostle who died at the Battle of Crooked River in 1838) and he wants me, and the Lord wants me, and I want to go.' They then gave him up.

"At one time as Joseph entered the room, he (Seymour) told him that there was a light encircled him above the brightness of the sun—he exclaimed, 'The room is full of angels, they have come to waft my spirit home.' He then bade his family and friends farewell and sweetly fell asleep in Jesus."[5] Later, in a written tribute, Elder Brunson was called a "lively stone in the building of God," and it was said that "he died in the triumph of faith."[6]

"Clothed in White"

Tears from deep emotions choked Daniel Tyler's grandfather as he told his family about the angel who had appeared to him and delivered a message. Daniel wrote about his grandfather's experience, which occurred in February, 1829.

"After my grand-father was taken with his last illness, he told my parents that an angel appeared to him clothed in white, and told him he would not recover, for his sickness was unto death. Ten days later he died. To save ridicule, however, this vision was kept secret and only told me afterwards by my mother. The true church of Christ was not then on the earth, nor had such an occurrence been heard of by us at the time. Although the Father and the Son had appeared to Joseph Smith some years previously, we had not heard of the vision. The vision of my grand-father seemed so strange that my parents hardly knew whether to attribute it to imagination or a reality, as they could not question his sincerity, he having always been strictly reliable. I have never doubted his having had the vision. After the vision, he walked half a mile to bid my parents good-by, although in poor health. On parting, my grand-father wept like a child, and said, 'This is the last time I shall ever visit you while I live."[7]

His Wife Was the First Person that Came to Him

Jedediah Grant was a loyal leader in the early church, serving as major-general of the Nauvoo Legion and later in the First Presidency as second counselor to Brigham Young. Near the end of his life, as Jedediah Grant lay near death, his spirit was transported to the spirit world. When his good friend, Heber C. Kimball came to see him, Jedediah told him about his spiritual experience. The following week, at Jedediah's funeral, which was held in December of 1856, President Kimball told the audience about his friend's experience.

President Kimball said, "He (Jedediah) saw the righteous gathered together in the spirit world, and there were no wicked spirits among them. He saw his wife; she was the first person that came to him. He saw many that he knew, but did not have conversation with any except his wife Caroline. She came to him, and he said that she looked beautiful and had their little child, that died on the Plains, in her arms, and said, 'Mr. Grant, here is little Margaret; you know that the wolves ate her up, but it did not hurt her; here she is all right.'

Jedediah continued, "To my astonishment, when I looked at families there was a deficiency in some, there was a lack, for I saw families that would not be permitted to come and dwell together, because they had not honored their calling here.'" He asked his wife Caroline where Joseph and Hyrum and Father Smith and others were; she replied, 'they have gone away ahead, to perform and transact business for us.'"[8]

"O, How Beautiful, But They Do Not Speak"

Mary Duty Smith, Joseph Smith's ninety-four-year-old grandmother, arrived at Kirtland for a visit, accompanied by two of her sons. Mary had asked the Lord to let her live to see her children and grandchildren one more time and in accordance with her wishes, her sons had brought her for a final visit. Although family members had told her about the restoration, Mary had not been baptized because her oldest son, Jesse, was bitterly opposed to the church.

However, when the aged lady arrived in Kirtland, she told Lucy, Joseph's mother, "I am going to have your Joseph baptize me, and my Joseph (the patriarch) bless me."[9]

Her husband, Israel, had been reading the Book of Mormon, but had died before finishing it. Israel had long stated his firm belief that a prophet would be raised up in his family and felt certain that his grandson Joseph was that prophet.

After her long journey to Kirtland, Mary was tired, but overjoyed to see two more of her sons, along with their many grandchildren and great-grandchildren. Unfortunately, the excitement seems to have been too much for a woman of advanced years and Mary became ill. She became feverish and her condition rapidly deteriorated until it became apparent that death was imminent. During the elderly woman's last hours, Eliza R. Snow stayed in Mary's bedroom, keeping watch.

Eliza states, "I was with her, and saw her calmly fall asleep. About ten minutes before she expired, she saw a group of angels in the room; and pointing towards them she exclaimed, 'O, how beautiful! But they do not speak.' It would seem that they were waiting to escort her spirit to its bright abode."[10]

"I Heard the Most Beautiful Singing"

Ella Jensen not only saw angels, but made a brief visit to where they lived. Ella became ill and passed away, but because her mission on earth had not yet been completed, she was sent back to earth after being summoned by Lorenzo Snow. Ella relates her extraordinary experience:

"On the 1st of March, 1891, I was taken severely ill with the scarlet fever, and suffered very much for a week. It was on the morning of the 9th that I awoke with a feeling that I was going to die. As soon as I opened my eyes I could see some of my relatives from the other world. They were engaged in conversation, and when they disappeared I heard the most beautiful singing, far superior to anything I had ever heard before. I then asked my sister to assist me in getting ready to go into the spirit world. She combed my hair, washed me, and I brushed my teeth and cleaned my nails that I might be clean when going before my Maker. All this time and for six hours, I could hear the singing still. I then bade my dear ones good by, and my spirit left my body.

"For some time I could hear my parents and relatives weeping and mourning, which troubled me greatly. As soon, however, as I had a glimpse of the other world my attention was drawn away from them to my relatives there, who all seemed pleased to see me. They were holding Sunday school, and Sister Eliza Snow was presiding. Everything was most lovely. Everybody was clothed in white. I saw so many of my departed friends and relatives . . . After having stayed with my departed friends what seemed to me but a very short time, yet it lasted several hours, I heard Apostle Lorenzo Snow administer to me, telling me that I must come back, as I had some work to do on the earth yet. I was loath to leave the heavenly place, but told my friends that I must leave them . . . I once more opened my eyes in this world of trouble and woe, and saw my beloved ones here."[11]

"A Halo of Light Surrounded the Personage"

Rebecca Reid's sickly grandmother had been bedfast for many years. Since her grandmother lived close by, Rebecca's parents frequently spent the night with her. One night a messenger came to Rebecca's house, informing the family that her grandmother was very ill. The children—including eight-year-old Rebecca—were told to stay at home, while her worried parents rushed off.

Rebecca said, "After what seemed a long time to me, I said to my brother and sisters, 'I am going to grandmother.' They tried their best to persuade me not to go; but I was determined. An irresistible something seemed to urge me forward. I was surprised at my own conduct, for I had always been obedient to my parents. So I opened the door and set out for the home of my grandmother.

"It was a very dark night in February. We lived in a village where there were no lights in the streets. In order to get to the house, I had to pass through a large gate, which was kept closed. I opened the gate, closed it behind me, and turned round to go to the house when I saw between two doorways the figure of an angel standing some distance from the ground, almost motionless. I was riveted to the spot, and stood gazing in astonishment at the strange sight.

"The appearance of the heavenly messenger denoted that she belonged to the female sex. She wore a drapery which passed over the shoulder and wound round the body. The feet and ankles were bare, as were also the hands and the greater part of the arms; the neck showed plainly. A halo of light, beautiful and bright, but not dazzling to the eyes, surrounded the personage. The figure began to move from side to side and to rise. It rose very slowly until it got above the building, when it entered a bright cloud and vanished from my sight.

"I awoke as from a dream. I rushed to the door of my grandmother's home. It was opened by my aunt, who told me to return home, that my grandma had just passed away. My father followed me soon afterwards. I told him and also my mother what I had seen, and father told me to not speak of it to anyone."[12]

Rebecca's amazing experience did not end there. As Rebecca grew older, she read avidly and listened carefully to speakers at funerals and lectures, hoping that someone would mention something similar to what she had seen on the night of her grandmother's death. But no one ever did. She remained puzzled, thinking that she couldn't be the only person to have seen an angel. Rebecca was also confused because she had been told that angels had wings but the personage she had seen looked just like a human being.

Years passed and Rebecca grew up. After a short association with the Church of England and Wesleyan Methodists, she joined the Society of Friends and was with them for sixteen years. Then, in the fall of 1905, a missionary for The Church of Jesus Christ of Latter-day Saints left a tract at her door. She quickly read it through and when the elder returned, invited him in. They had a lively discussion. Intrigued by what she heard, Rebecca began investigating the church. She was pleased that the Church's doctrine corresponded with the teachings of Christ and His apostles and was in perfect harmony with her own beliefs. Reading the account of Joseph's Smith's first vision made a great impact on her. As Rebecca pondered upon Joseph's words, she felt certain that he spoke the truth. It was at that moment that the angel she had seen so many years before, reappeared.

Rebecca testified; "The heavenly messenger I saw the night my grandmother died stood some distance from the ground. I was convinced in my heart and soul that Joseph spoke the truth. I felt that I could understand his feelings when he said, 'Why persecute me for telling the truth? I have actually seen a vision, and who am I that I can withstand

God, or why does the world think to make me deny what I have actually seen?' It was the same in my own case: I had actually seen a messenger from the unseen world; I knew that I had, and no one could
convince me I had not."

Rebecca decided at that moment to join the church. The appearance
of the angel not only blessed her spiritually but physically as well. In an
interesting footnote to her story, Rebecca states, "Prior to that time I suffered much from ill health; but after my baptism I was returned to perfect health, which has continued down to the present time."[13]

"The Angel of the Lord Visited Him"

Alvin Smith, brother of the prophet and the oldest son of Joseph
Smith Senior and Lucy Mack Smith, died on November 19, 1823.
Although he passed away before the church was organized, Alvin was
alive when the angel Moroni visited his brother. He encouraged Joseph
to be faithful and do everything the angel told him.

Joseph Smith said that his brother, Alvin, saw an angel just before
he died. Joseph wrote:

"Alvin, my oldest brother—I remember well the pangs of sorrow
that swelled my youthful bosom and almost burst my tender heart when
he died. He was one of the noblest sons of men. Shall his name not be
recorded in this book (i.e. The Book of the Law of the Lord). Yes, Alvin,
let it be had there and be handed down upon these sacred pages for ever
and ever. In him there was no guile. He lived without spot from the time
he was a child. From the time of his birth he never knew mirth. He was
candid and sober and never would play; and minded his father and
mother in toiling all day. He was one of the soberest of men, and when
he died the angel of the Lord visited him in his last moments." [14]

"I See Alvin!"

When Joseph Smith Senior—father of the prophet—died, he was
welcomed at the threshold of heaven by a special angel—his son, Alvin,
who had died many years before. Made feeble by his advanced years
and further weakened by illness, Joseph's health seriously declined during the first months of 1840. During the spring, he was often confined
to bed and when summer arrived, his health deteriorated still further.

On September 14, 1840, Joseph began vomiting blood. Sensing that the end was near, his wife, Lucy, sent for Joseph, Hyrum and their other children. Although barely able to speak, Joseph pronounced one last blessing on each of his children. After resting a bit, he then spoke to his wife, telling her not to mourn at his death. Lucy recorded what happened next:

"He then paused for some time, being exhausted. After which he said, in a tone of surprise, 'I can see and hear, as well as ever I could.' (A second pause of considerable length.) 'I see Alvin.' (Third pause.) 'I shall live seven or eight minutes.' Then straightening himself, he laid his hands together; after which he began to breathe shorter, and in about eight minutes his breath stopped, without even a struggle or a sigh, and his spirit took its flight for the regions where the justified ones rest from their labors. He departed so calmly, that, for some time, we could not believe but that he would breathe again."[15]

He Saw Joseph and Hyrum

As a young man, Alexander Neibaur saw a newly translated book of scripture in a vision and was impressed that the new book had been brought forth by the power of God. Because of that vision, when Alexander heard that Joseph Smith had seen an angel and translated a book of scripture, he knew without a doubt that this 'new' religion was true.

Alexander was one of the first Jews to accept the newly restored gospel and shortly after his conversion, he sailed to America. Upon his arrival in Nauvoo, in February of 1841, he became friends with the Prophet Joseph. Alexander was a very educated man, able to speak seven languages and began teaching the prophet German and Hebrew.

Alexander fled Nauvoo with the Saints and traveled across the plains. His testimony of the gospel and the divine calling of Joseph Smith remained firm throughout the years of hardships and in the last moments of his life, he had the privilege to once again behold his dear friend Joseph, as well as his brother Hyrum. Several of Alexander's children were with him during his last hours on earth. In a feeble voice, Alexander related the many difficult trials he had faced because of his membership in the church.

One son then asked, "'Father, you have been telling us of your long and hard experience . . . But let me ask you, is it worth it all? Is the Gospel worth all this sacrifice?'"

A glow lit Alexander's eyes and he spoke firmly, "'Yes! Yes! And more! I have seen my Savior. I have seen the prints in his hands! I know that Jesus is the son of God, and I know that this work is true and that Joseph Smith was a prophet of God. I would suffer it all and more, far more than I have ever suffered for that knowledge even to the laying down of my body on the plains for the wolves to devour.'"

The account then states that, ". . . a short time before the end, his face suddenly lit up and his countenance brightened. He cast his eyes upward as if he could see far into upper distant spaces.

"'What do you see, father?' they asked.

"The dying man murmured clearly, 'Joseph—Hyrum'—then his weary eyes closed forever."[16]

Angels All Around

In the fall of 1833, a preacher came to the Latter-day Saint settlement in Independence, Jackson County to buy guns. He claimed that he wanted them for protection against the Indians, but shortly after, the Saints heard that armed mobs were assembling and making threats to drive them from the county. Two men, Philo Dibble and John Poorman, hurriedly went to nearby Liberty to purchase ammunition for the few guns they had left. Shortly after their return, a mob of about one hundred and fifty men descended on the settlement, tearing down houses, and whipping and beating the men.

The fighting lasted several days. In the final battle, the mob was routed but several brethren were shot. One of the men, named Barber, was mortally wounded. The account states:

"After the battle was over, some of the brethren went to administer to him, but he objected to their praying that he might live, and asked them if they could not see the angels present. He said the room was full of them, and his greatest anxiety was for his friends to see what he saw, until he breathed his last, which occurred at three o'clock in the morning."[17]

Notes for Part Eight

1 Joseph F. Smith, *Conference Report,* April 1916, p. 3.

2 Aurelia Spencer Rogers, *Life Sketches of Orson Spencer and Others,* (Salt Lake City: George Q. Cannon & Sons Company, 1898), pp. 36-37.

3 *Ibid.,* pp. 37-38.

4 *Ibid.,* p. 39.

5 Helen Mar Whitney, "Scenes and Incidents in Nauvoo," *Woman's Exponent,* vol. 10, 15 March 1882, p. 159.

6 *Journal History of the Church,* 10 August 1840, p. 179.

7 Daniel Tyler, "Incidents of Experience," *Scraps of Biography, Tenth Book of the Faith Promoting Series,* (Salt Lake City: Juvenile Instructor Office, 1883), p. 23.

8 Heber C. Kimball, *Journal of Discourses,* vol. 4, p. 136.

9 Edward Tullidge, *The Women of Mormondom* (New York: 1877), p. 98.

10 *Ibid.,* pp. 98-99.

11 Ella Jensen, "Remarkable Experience," *Young Woman's Journal,* vol. 4, January 1893, p. 165.

12 Rebecca Reid, "My Introduction to 'Mormonism,'" *Latter-day Saints' Millennial Star,* vol. 70, 6 August, 1908, pp. 501-502.

13 *Ibid.,* p. 503.

14 Joseph Fielding Smith, *Life of Joseph F. Smith,* (Salt Lake City: The Deseret News Press, 1938), p. 38.

15 Lucy Mack Smith, *History of Joseph Smith, by His Mother, Lucy Mack Smith,* (Salt Lake City: Stevens & Wallis, 1945), pp. 313-14.

16 *Utah Genealogical and Historical Magazine,* vol. V, April 1914, p. 62.

17 *Early Scenes in Church History, Eighth Book of the Faith Promoting Series,* (Salt Lake City: Juvenile Instructor Office, 1882), pp. 82-83.

Part Nine
Angels Protecting from Harm

Brigham Young testified that God sends angels to defend those in need of protection. He declared, "The Lord is here with us, not in person, but his angels are around us, and he takes cognizance of every act of the children of men, as individuals and as nations. He is here ready by his agents, the angels, and by the power of his Holy spirit and Priesthood, which he has restored in these last days, to bring most perfect and absolute deliverance unto all who put their trust in Him."[1]

Insofar as mortals are able, we are encouraged to help those around us. However, we may be unaware of another's plight or for various other reasons, unable to help. When no other source of relief is in sight, angels may be sent to assist those in need. In a discourse to the Saints, Heber C. Kimball once said, "Do you suppose that there are any angels here to-day? I would not wonder if there were ten times more angels here than people. We do not see them, but they are here watching us, and are anxious for our salvation . . . The Lord has hosts of angels who are qualified to defend us . . ."[2]

We have a right to ask Heavenly Father to safeguard us. In the Book of Mormon, we read that the people called upon God, asking Him to ". . . protect this people in righteousness, so long as they shall call on the name of their God for protection." (3 Nephi 4:30) Brigham Young told the Saints to instruct their children to ask God to watch over them. He said, "Teach the children to pray, that when they are large enough to go into the field with their father, they may have faith that if they are in danger, they will be protected. Teach them that those good angels that are ministering spirits, and their angels, to guard and defend the just and pure, watch over them continually." (as quoted in, *Looking for Angels,* p. 31)

The scriptures relate many times when angels have been sent to protect God's people. When Sennacherib, the king of Assyria, invaded Judah, Hezekiah spoke to his people comfortingly, saying, "Be strong and courageous, be not afraid nor dismayed for the king of Assyria, nor for all the multitude that is with him: for there be more with us than with him: With him is an arm of flesh; but with us is the Lord our God to help us, and to fight our battles . . . And the Lord sent an angel, which cut off all the mighty men of valour, and the leaders and captains in the camp of the king of Assyria . . . Thus the Lord saved Hezekiah and the inhabitants of Jerusalem." (2 Chronicles 32:7-8, 21-22)

Angels are sometimes dispatched to preserve the life of persons who have not yet fulfilled their earthly missions and are not appointed unto death. The apostle Marriner Wood Merrill, who was once saved from certain death by an unseen power said, "I can truthfully testify in all soberness, that some power which I did not see assisted me from the position which would speedily have cost me my life. As I was preserved for some purpose known to my heavenly Father, so do I also believe that God will bless and preserve the lives of His faithful children . . . and He will, if necessary send angelic visitors to sustain and preserve those who put their trust in Him."[3] Although mortal eyes usually cannot detect the angel that is protecting them from injury or death, the following accounts relate a few occasions when people have been blessed to see their angelic protector.

Sent by Her Departed Father

Born in Devonshire, England, Elizabeth Drake Davis was an only child. Having lost her father when she was ten and not being close to her mother, Elizabeth often felt very alone as she was growing up. One day, as she was praying about her loneliness, she was shown a vision, which led her to the Church of Jesus Christ of Latter-day Saints. Elizabeth was taught the gospel, gained a testimony and was baptized. She later married and had two little girls. When her husband died unexpectedly, Elizabeth scraped together enough money to come to America.

She lived for several years in Philadelphia, saving every spare penny so she could travel west and join the Saints in Salt Lake City. When Elizabeth had enough money saved, she traveled to Florence and joined the small group of Saints with whom she would travel across the plains. While Elizabeth was there, she had a wondrous experience.

Elizabeth relates; "We reached Florence late one evening; it was quite dark and raining; we were helped from the wagons and put in one of the vacant houses—myself, my two little daughters and Sister Sarah White. Early next morning we were aroused by someone knocking at the door; on opening it we found a little girl with a cup of milk in her hand; she asked if there was 'a little woman there with two little children.'

"'Yes,' said Sister White. 'Come in.'

"She entered, saying to me, 'If you please my ma wants to see you; she has sent this milk to your little girls.'

"Her mother's name was strange to me, but I went, thinking to find some one that I had known. She met me at the door with both hands extended in welcome.

"'Good morning, Sister Elizabeth,' said she. I told her she had the advantage of me, as I did not remember ever seeing her before.

"'No,' said she, 'and I never saw you before. I am Hyrum Smith's daughter (Lovina Walker); and my father appeared to me three times last night, and told me that you were a child of God, that you was without money, provisions or friends, and that I must help you.'"

No doubt Elizabeth was comforted to know that spirits on the other side were keeping watch over her. Grateful for Lovina's help, she declared, "It is needless to add that this excellent lady and myself were ever thereafter firm friends."[4]

Although Elizabeth and Lovina became good friends, they lost track of each other as the years passed. Later in life however, Elizabeth was given the opportunity to bless her friend's life as Lovina had once blessed hers, in a way that was uncannily similar to the long-ago incident in Florence. Once again a loving father, Hyrum Smith, appeared to procure assistance for someone in need. But this time he appeared to Elizabeth and asked her to go and help his own daughter, Lovina, who was in desperate need of help.

Elizabeth relates, "I will add that previous to her last illness I had not seen her in thirteen years; that one night her father appeared to me, and making himself known, said his daughter was in sore need; I found the message was too true."

Elizabeth went quickly to Lovina and finding her in dire straits, was able to help her old friend. Elizabeth concludes this experience by stating, "Yet it will ever be a source of gratitude to think I was at least able to return her generous kindness to me when we were strangers."5

Dragged from the Railroad Tracks

When Christopher Elias Jensen and his brother, Lorenzo, were hired to work on the Oregon Short Line Railroad, they both knew the job was dangerous. They were both brakemen—a job that could be very hazardous. Prior to working on the railroad, Christopher had not been in the habit of praying but because of the risks he would now be facing daily, decided that it was a good time to start. The young man began calling upon Heavenly Father to protect him and preserve his life while he labored for the railroad. In return, he promised to live righteously, abstain from tobacco and liquor and never take God's name in vain. Christopher kept his word and in 1898, God kept His—sending a very familiar angel to save the young man's life.

Christopher recounts the incident: "While going north on one of our trips, we stopped at the station of Collinston, about twenty miles north of Brigham City. We were doing some switching of the cars. I was on top of a large furniture car giving signals to the engineer while my brother, Lorenzo, and another brakeman by the name of Hill, were cutting the cars. My brother was attending the switch and Mr. Hill was between two of the cars making an effort to uncouple the cars. He failed to get the cars uncoupled, and, thinking that something had happened to him, I ran across the top of the car to see what was the matter. The cars were still traveling at a fast rate of speed and as I approached the end of the car where Mr. Hill was working, the engineer suddenly reversed the engine brakes, which caused it to stop very suddenly. It uncoupled the cars and sent me headlong from the top of the car to the ground where I fell on my back across the rails.

"The train immediately proceeded again in the direction it was going and was within a very few feet of where I lay. I cannot say how I ever got off the track, for I was unconscious, but my brother, who was standing at the switch a short distance from where I lay, testifies that he saw our father suddenly appear and take me by the shoulders, drag me from the track and lay me down on the ground a few feet from where my brother stood—the cars by this time having passed over the spot where I had lain. It will be remembered that my father had died in the preceding July and this incident happened during the month of December of the same year."[6]

"I Saw the Hand of the Angel"

Lorenzo Young, a brother of Brigham Young, was blessed to see angels twice during his life. The first time, an angel came to his rescue when the Saints fought a lawless mob during the Battle of Crooked River.

In the months prior to this battle, the Saints had been persecuted unmercifully. Even though church members obeyed their leaders who asked them not to retaliate against their tormentors, depredations against the Saints increased. Conditions finally became intolerable when the mob captured two men. The two brethren were unlawfully tried by a mock court and found guilty. When word reached the Saints that the two men were condemned to be shot the following morning at eight, plans were hastily made to rescue them.

That evening, David W. Patten, one of the twelve apostles (who was later killed in the battle) gathered together a company of forty men, including Lorenzo Young. They spent a tense night making plans. Then, in the early morning darkness, a bass drum sounded, signaling the time had come to take up arms and free their brethren. The men mounted their horses and rode to Crooked River.

As the sun began peeking over the horizon, the Saints dismounted near the enemy camp. They were walking cautiously down the road, squinting into the rising sun, when suddenly, the sharp crack of a rifle shattered the stillness of the morning. Brother Obanion, who was just one step in front of Lorenzo, fell to the ground. Men shouted as more shots rang out. Lorenzo and John P. Green carried Obanion to a safer spot by the side of the road, then charged into the melee.

As they neared the river, the firing became intense. The order to charge was given and as the brethren surged forward, the enemy broke and ran. Lorenzo fired, then stopped to reprime his gun. A short distance away, he saw a tall, powerful Missourian spring out from under a bank. With a heavy sword in hand, the enemy rushed toward a man who was all by himself. Fearing that the lone man, who was much smaller than his attacker, would be totally overpowered, Lorenzo ran to his aid.

When he was close enough to get off a shot, Lorenzo stopped and leveled his gun. The Missourian, seeing the danger he was in, stopped his charge and ducked but the rifle misfired. He then turned away from his intended victim and charged Lorenzo. Brother Young had saved the other man's life but in doing so, had placed himself in peril.

Lorenzo admits that his situation was dangerous. "The Missourian turned on me. With nothing but the muzzle end of my rifle to parry his rapid blows, my situation was perilous. The man whom I had relieved, for some reason, did not come to the rescue. I succeeded in parrying the blows of my enemy until he backed me to the bank of the river. I could back no farther without going off the perpendicular bank, eight or ten feet above the water. In a moment, I realized that my chances were very desperate.

"At this juncture, the Missourian raised his sword, apparently throwing all his strength and energy into the act, as if intending to crush me with one desperate blow. As his arm extended, I saw a hand pass down the back of his head and between his shoulders. There was no other person visible and I have always believed that I saw the hand of the angel of the Lord interposed for my deliverance. The arm of my enemy was paralyzed, and I had time to extricate myself from the perilous situation I was in. I do not see how I could have been saved in the way I was, without a providential interference."[7]

Lorenzo's second experience with an angel occurred after he was injured while working as a blacksmith. He relates:

"For some time my health continued poor. One day I lay on a bed to rest where I could see the family in their ordinary occupations. All at once I heard the most beautiful music. I soon discovered from whence it came. Standing side by side, on the foot board of the bed stead on which I lay, were two beautiful, seraph-like beings, about the size of children seven or eight years old. They were dressed in white and appeared surpassingly pure and heavenly. I felt certain that I was fully awake, and these juvenile personages were realistic to me. With their disappearance the music ceased. I turned and asked two of my sisters, who were in the room, if they had not heard the music. I was much surprised to lean that they had heard nothing."[8]

"Miraculously Saved from a Shocking Death"

Orson Smith, a young man who later became president of the Cache Stake, was so surprised to hear an angel's voice that he did not immediately obey the angel's command. The angelic order was then repeated and accompanied with a physical shaking that compelled the young man to obey, and saved his life.

The experience occurred in 1868, when Orson was working at a sawmill that was owned in part by his father. He had been learning how to operate the mill since returning home from a mission a short time before. As the weather turned colder in late fall, certain precautions needed to be taken at the end of the day's work. To prevent the mill race from bursting during the night, when water would freeze and expand, Orson closed the gate at the head of the race and opened the gate of the Leffel water wheel to let the water drain out.

One frosty fall morning, Orson went to the mill and opened the gate lever, which was supposed to close the wheel gate. He then went to the head gate, let the water in and returned to the mill and started filing the circular saw. It was Orson's customary practice to put his left leg over the saw frame as he filed, which brought his left thigh close to the saw.

Orson reported, "I had proceeded with my task but a few moments when an audible voice said to me, 'Get up.' I knew no other person was in the mill. Still I hesitated and looked around as if to see who was speaking to me. I made another stroke with my file, when I was aroused by the same voice in a louder tone and such a perceptible shaking of my body, as if some power had hold of me, that I was compelled to rise.

"I had no sooner become disentangled from the saw teeth than it started at full speed. The wheel gates had frozen to the rim of the wheel, and had not closed as they should have done, thus causing the entire current to rush through the wheel; not until the water had thawed the ice from the gates would they close, but just as soon as they were released the wheel started at full speed. Had not the warning come to me as it did, my body would have been sawed asunder, as I was totally ignorant of the danger to which I was exposed. It was some time before I could return to my work, so great was the shock upon me, when I saw how miraculously I had been delivered from a shocking death."[9]

"They Saw an Angel on Each End of the House"

While living in Independence, Missouri, members of the Church of Jesus Christ faced bitter persecution from mobs, but on at least one occasion, the violence was halted when angels intervened.

When Mary Elizabeth Rollins was ten years old, her family moved to Kirtland, Ohio and in the fall of 1831, they relocated to Independence. While there, the Saints were subjected to terrible persecution as mobs destroyed buildings and set fire to grain and haystacks, leaving them in ashes. Many brethren, including Bishop Partridge and

Charles Allen were tarred and feathered. The mob destroyed the church's printing press and ransacked the office, tossing pages of the Book of Commandments out of the window onto the street below. Mary and her sister Caroline managed to snatch up some of the pages and when mobbers chased them, ran and hid themselves and the priceless pages in a cornfield.

Uncontrolled mobs roved the streets, stoning the houses and breaking down doors and windows. One frightening evening, they besieged Mary's home. Mary recalled; "One night a great many men got together and stoned our house, part of which was hewed logs, the other part or front was brick. After breaking all the windows, they started tearing off the roof on the brick part amidst awful oaths and yells that were terrible to hear. We were all frightened and stood against the walls between the doors and windows. All at once they stopped and all was quiet. Some of the Brethren who were on the way to see if they could help us said they saw an angel resting on each gable end of our house, so that must have been the reason."[10]

An Angelic Army

While the Saints were in Kirtland, Joseph Smith recorded that his scribe saw a wonderful vision, where the Lord sent an angelic army to earth to protect His people.

He stated; "My scribe also received his anointing with us, (the presidency of the church) and saw, in a vision, the armies of heaven protecting the Saints in their return to Zion . . ."[11]

Joseph's scribe was not the only one to see heavenly armies watching over the people. It was recorded that, "President William Smith, one of the Twelve, saw the heavens opened, and the Lord's host protecting the Lord's anointed."[12]

"Angels Went Before Us"

In an attempt to obtain government aid for members of the church who had been driven out of their homes by persecution, Joseph Smith met with Governor Dunklin. The governor pledged to use the militia to restore the people to their homes if the Saints could gather together a large enough force to keep them in Missouri. To receive the state's aid, Joseph Smith assembled over 200 armed men in May of 1834 and led them to Missouri; an 1800-mile round trip that came to be called Zion's Camp.

In a revelation given to the prophet, the Lord testified that he would send angels to help the men of Zion's Camp. "Therefore, let not your hearts faint, for I say not unto you as I said unto your fathers: Mine angel shall go up before you, but not my presence. But I say unto you: Mine angels shall go up before you, and also my presence . . ." (D&C 103:19-20)

Heber C. Kimball, Orson Pratt, Joseph Smith and other men in Zion's Camp verified that the Lord's promise was fulfilled. Heber C. Kimball stated in his journal that the brethren who made the long journey to aid the beleaguered Saints were protected by heavenly sources as they traveled. Heber wrote; "On the 26th we resumed our journey. At night we were alarmed by the continual threatening of our enemies. I would here remark that notwithstanding so many threats were thrown out against us, we did not fear nor hesitate to proceed on our journey, for God was with us, and angels went before us, and we had no fear of either men or devils. This we know because angels were seen."[13]

Although the men of Zion's Camp did not always live up to what was expected of them, they were blessed on many different occasions by the hand of the Lord. Joseph Smith said that heavenly angels protected them on their journey. On May 27, 1834, he wrote, "Notwithstanding our enemies were breathing threats of violence, we did not fear, neither did we hesitate to prosecute our journey, for God was with us, and his angels were before us, and the faith of our little band was unwavering."[14]

Orson Pratt, another member of Zion's Camp, declared; "After we were organized we pursued our journey and received instructions from time to time, of Joseph, who was appointed to lead the camp of Israel; and behold the presence of the Lord was with us by day and by night and his angel went before us to prepare the way."[15]

Angel with a Sword

On January 28, 1836, Roger Orton saw a vision, which showed angels protecting the Saints. Joseph Smith recorded it as follows: ". . . Elder Roger Orton saw a mighty angel riding upon a horse of fire, with a flaming sword in his hand, followed by five others, encircle the house, and protect the Saints, even the Lord's anointed, from the power of Satan and a host of evil spirits, which were striving to disturb the Saints."[16]

About this same time in Kirtland, Joseph saw a vision of an angel protecting Brigham Young. Joseph records; "Also, I saw Elder

Brigham Young standing in a strange land, in the far south and west, in a desert place, upon a rock in the midst of about a dozen men of color, who appeared hostile. He was preaching to them in their own tongue, and the angel of God standing above his head, with a drawn sword in his hand, protecting him, but he did not see it."[17]

"Angels of God Would Go Before Them"

Angry mobs threatened that if the Saints stayed in Illinois, they would face death by fire, sword and gun. However, to leave without making adequate preparations meant death by cold and starvation. As it turned out, the people decided they had no choice but to abandon their homes and flee for their lives. As the Saints made hasty preparations to leave and cross the territory of Iowa, they gathered together on Sunday, the first day of March in 1846, to receive instructions from church leaders. Jane B. Taylor listened as the beleaguered Saints were given the promise of angelic help during their journey.

Jane recorded in her journal; "Bro. Kimball exhorted the Saints to be diligent in prayer to Almighty God all the day long. He called especially upon heads of families to attend daily to family worship, and to give heed to counsel, assuring them that if they did so God would bless them, and angels of God would go before them and would be the breakers up of our way."[18]

"Thy Guardian Angel Hath Watched Over Thee"

Truman Angell was appointed superintendent over the joiner work on the Nauvoo Temple, under the direction of architect William Weeks. When William fled Nauvoo, along with the twelve apostles, Truman was left to finish the lower hall by himself. Even though staying in the beleaguered city put him in danger, Truman was determined to complete work on the temple.

When the temple was done, Truman traveled across the plains and shortly after his arrival in Salt Lake City, was chosen to be the architect for the church. For years, he was kept busy designing and managing the construction of numerous buildings. While Truman was overseeing work on the St. George temple, he felt prompted to obtain his patriarchal blessing and approached Patriarch John Smith with his request. Truman was told in his blessing that angels had protected him many times during his life and that an angel would continue to protect him.

In part, the blessing proclaimed: "Thou are of Joseph out of the loins of Ephraim, and entitled to all the blessings promised to his posterity by his father, Jacob, because of thine integrity. Thy guardian Angel hath watched over thee and borne thee up in times of danger, and preserved thy life from enemies both seen and unseen, and will continue to do so all thy days."[19]

"You'd Better Go!"

It was on the evening of March 28, 1890, that Elder Henry S. Tanner first heard the voice of an angel. It happened when he and Elder David T. LeBaron—who was president of the South Carolina Conference (Mission)—were at the home of John Gordon, who lived near Gaffney, South Carolina. Although the elders knew that there had been a forest fire nearby that day, they didn't know that after the men extinguished it, they had gathered at a local church and talk about the fire had turned to a discussion on how to exterminate the Mormons. However, God was aware of the mob spirit and sent an angel to warn the missionaries.

Just before dinner that night, Elder Tanner heard a distinct voice say, "You'd better go." He looked around but saw no one. Becoming nervous and uncomfortable, he suggested to Elder LeBaron that they leave. His companion—unable to see any danger in staying—dismissed his fears as groundless, pointing out that they were among friends and that there were a number of Latter-day Saint families near by.

Elder Tanner stated, "A second and a third time I heard the voice, and each time went to my companion and told him what I had heard and how I felt. Brother LeBaron, who was always very deliberate, and knew no fear, thought it somewhat inconsistent for us to leave our friends, hoping to find security elsewhere . . ."[20]

As the evening progressed, Elder Tanner felt increasingly worried and upset. Finally, a vision opened to him. He saw a crowd of men coming from the road. They surrounded the house and lifted up stones to throw at the door and window.

Suddenly, in reality, there was a series of loud thuds as rocks crashed against the house. Everyone in the house jumped up as the mob burst through the door. The men of the mob leveled their rifles at the missionaries and told them to come with them. The elders were marched down the road and when they came to a fork in the road, were dismayed to see another large group of men waiting. The mob spouted vulgar and thunderous oaths as they stripped the missionaries of their coats, vests and shirts. Then they began beating the defenseless men with hickory sticks. In the midst of the attack, Elder Tanner thought about the promise that had been given him before leaving on his mission, which promised that he would go in peace and return in safety.

He thought, "Lord you made a mistake this time."

Immediately the words came back, "You did not obey the Spirit of the Lord."

Henry said that after hearing that rebuke and knowing it to be true, he "fairly wilted, offering a secret prayer for forgiveness and deliverance." Finally the mob decided to let the bruised and battered missionaries go, telling them to leave quickly.

Elder Tanner said, "We had no sooner started than they tried to recall us, but in pursuance of their other order we 'hit the grit.' Thus thwarted in their design, they began to throw stones and shoot at us. A great number of shots were fired, and bullets and missiles fell all around, but not one hit us. Thus we were delivered from the mob, and by following the whispering of the Spirit always after avoided them."

The second time an angel warned Elder Tanner, he was quicker to obey. He relates his second experience, saying; "Within a week of the above occurrence and at about nine o'clock at night, we were warned as before, and as soon as we could tell the folks good by and pick up our grips we commenced to travel. As we were leaving the yard a friend came running and told us to go quickly for a mob was coming. As we left the clearing on one side, the mob entered on the other, thus we missed an entangling alliance."[21]

That experience was not to be the last time Elder Tanner heard an angelic voice during his mission. In September of 1892, while he was in Pireway, North Carolina, preparing for conference, he heard another angel speak.

Elder Tanner states, "Early in the morning, when I was returning from the woods where I had been in prayer, a voice said, 'Go to Long Bay.' I looked around but could see no one. The words were repeated and I felt a power accompanying them. I was considerably agitated and began to wonder why I was told to go to Long Bay. During my meditation the words were repeated, 'Go to Long Bay,' and I answered, 'I'll go.'

"I went immediately to the house of Monroe Long, where I was staying, and asked for the use of his horse and buggy to drive to Long

Bay. Mr. Long wished to know what I was going to Long Bay for, and I told him that I did not know except that I felt impressed to go there, to which he answered, 'You "Mormons" get funnier all the time; I can't understand you.' However, he lent me his horse and buggy and I proceeded to Long Bay."

Henry drove to the home of John Patrick and when no one answered his knock, opened the door and walked inside. No one was in the front room, so he went through the house and into a bedroom located at the rear of the house. To his astonishment, there were two sick men lying in bed; Elders Henry D. Wallace, and James S. Carlyle. They were both suffering from malaria. Not once had Henry thought of elders being in the area. The last he had heard of these two missionaries was that they were in another area.

Elder Tanner said, "I went to each of the elders in turn, took them by the hands and commanded them to arise in the name of Jesus Christ, and be made whole. They arose and dressed; and rejoiced because the power of God had been made manifest in their behalf."[22]

"Surrounded by a Circle of Personages"

In 1882, many powerful and influential people in Washington were very opposed to and openly antagonistic toward the Latter-day Saints in Utah. As a result, George Q. Cannon, who held a seat in Congress, had to face a tremendous amount of hostility. In fact, there was so much enmity that many people became anxious about Elder Cannon's safety.

One morning while in the St. George temple, David Cannon—George's brother—confided his fears to Brother John D. T. McAllister. David declared that he felt that the same feeling and spirit that had caused the martyrdom of Joseph and Hyrum at Carthage, now existed in Washington and was directed towards his brother.

Later that morning, David was called upon to give the opening prayer and asked for a special blessing to be upon his brother, George. Minerva W. Snow was present during the invocation and saw an extraordinary spiritual manifestation. M.F. Farnsworth recorded her experience:

"A large room—like unto the halls of Congress, was presented to her view, filled with many men, nicely clad, and arranged at their various places in the body of the hall. Their eyes were upon Brother George Q., who stood conspicuously on a platform with his right arm raised to heaven. He seemed to be pleading with this body of men. As she looked, she saw that he was surrounded by a circle of personages clothed in white, who by their presence prevented anyone from reaching him. She thus knew that his safety was assured, and so expressed herself that no further anxiety for him need be felt, for he was well protected."[23]

"Whenever You Are in Danger, I Will Come"

Elder Tom Shreeve was in New Zealand when he decided—on the 27th of February, 1879—to go to North Island. He was hoping to open up the area to missionary work, but after a time, he became anxious and despondent, remembering that all attempts to bring the gospel to the area in the past had failed. The dark feelings increased until Elder Shreeve began to doubt his ability to accomplish any good in the area at all. He then had the following experience:

"While I lay, wide awake, in my bed I suddenly saw a hand and arm, clothed in a white sleeve which extended down midway between the elbow and the wrist, and holding a torch in its hand—thrust out from the side of a dark fireplace which was in the room. At first there was but a spark of light at the top of the torch, but gradually the flame grew greater and the light stronger, until it filled the whole room; and then from out the darkness behind the arm and torch stepped the figure of a little girl.

"I recognized it instantly as that of my young sister Sophia, who had died six years before in England, while I was in Utah. At the time of her death she was eight and a half years old, and had but recently been baptized into the Church. She came toward the bed, and I saw that she was dressed in beautiful white raiment. From her whole person a pleasing light seemed to emanate. She approached the bed and leaned over it, placing her arms around my neck and kissing me upon the lips. Then, still with her hands clasped, she leaned back and looked intently into my face, saying at the same time:

"'Tom, don't be afraid! Whenever you are in danger I will come to warn you.'"

"She bent forward and kissed me again; afterward leaning back to take another look at my face. Repeating the same words as before, once more she kissed me; and then slowly withdrew her arms and moved back from the bed. She approached the arm, which still held the torch, and as she did so I saw that the light of the torch paled before the greater glory which surrounded her person. When she neared the fireplace the arm stretched out around her, and she stepped back into the darkness.

"She waved her hand three times with a farewell gesture toward me. Soon she was enveloped in the darkness of the fireplace, and the light of the torch grew for a moment brighter; then suddenly it vanished and I found myself leaning upon my elbow in the bed and gazing fixedly at the blank darkness where the glorious presence and the light torch had disappeared. So real and certain had been the presence of my sister that after she was gone I still felt the pressure of her warm arms around my neck."[24]

Notes for Part Nine

1   Brigham Young, *Journal of Discourses,* vol. 11, p. 14.
2   Heber C. Kimball, *Journal of Discourses,* vol. 3, March 2, 1856, p. 230.
3   Marriner Wood Merrill, *Juvenile Instructor,* 15 October 1892, p. 630.
4   Edward Tullidge, *The Women of Mormondom* (New York, 1877), pp. 451-52.
5   *Ibid.* p. 452.
6   *Ancestry and Descendants of Mads Christian Jensen,* 1600-1960, (Salt Lake City: LDS Church Archives), pp. 393-94.
7   Lorenzo Young, *Fragments of Experience, Sixth Book of the Faith Promoting Series,* (Salt Lake City: Juvenile Instructor Office, 1882), pp. 51-52.
8   *Ibid.,* p. 27.
9   Orson Smith, "How Others Have Risen," *Juvenile Instructor,* vol. 31, 1896, p. 18.
10 Mary Elizabeth Rollins Lightner [1936], (Unpublished manuscript, Salt Lake City: LDS Church Archives), p. 6.
11 Joseph Smith, *History of The Church of Jesus Christ of Latter-day Saints,* Period 1, vol. II, (Salt Lake City: Deseret News, 1904), p. 381.
12 Joseph Smith, Jr., compiled by Leland R. Nelson, *The Journal of Joseph,* (Provo: Council Press, 1979), p. 106.
13 Helen Mar Whitney, "Life Incidents," *Woman's Exponent,* vol. 9, 15 September 1880, p. 15.

14 M. F. Farnsworth, "Temple Manifestations," *The Contributor,* vol. 16, (Salt Lake City: Deseret News Publishing Co., 1895), pp. 65-66.

15 *The Orson Pratt Journals,* compiled by Elden J. Watson (Salt Lake City: LDS Church History Library, 1975), p. 40.

16 Joseph Smith, Jr., *The Journal of Joseph,* compiled by Leland R. Nelson, *op cit.,* p. 106.

17 Joseph Smith, *History of The Church of Jesus Christ of Latter-day Saints,* Period 1, vol. II, *op cit.,* p. 381.

18 *Woman's Exponent,* vol. 12, 1 December 1883, pp. 102-103.

19 Truman Angell, *Our Pioneer Heritage,* vol. 10, compiled by Kate B. Carter (Salt Lake City: Utah Printing Co., 1967), p. 201.

20 Henry S. Tanner, "For the Increase of Faith," *Improvement Era,* Part 2, vol. 11, May 1908, pp. 535-36.

21 *Ibid.,* p. 537.

22 *Ibid.,* pp. 538-39.

23 Joseph Smith, *History of the Church,* vol. II (Salt Lake City: Deseret News Press, third ed. 1961), p. 73.

24 *Helpful Visions, the Fourteenth Book of the Faith Promoting Series,* (Salt Lake City: 1887), pp. 68-69.

Part Ten
Angels at Temple Dedications

The veil that God has set in place to separate heaven and earth often conceals angels from our view, so that even when spiritual beings are near, we are not likely to be aware of their presence. However, there are special circumstances and certain holy places where and when the veil is more likely to become thin or even disappear altogether. The temple is one of those places.

Temples are sacred places—sanctuaries where God can abide—and they provide a special conduit between heaven and earth. The highest and most sacred ordinances of the gospel are performed within temple walls, the effects of which are binding for the living and the dead. Because of the holy and significant nature of temples, it is certain that angels are often present in those sacred structures.

The collective joy in heaven at the dedication of a temple often cannot be suppressed, resulting in many marvelous spiritual manifestations. Spirits on the other side of the veil are well aware of events occurring on earth and when a temple is dedicated, there is exultation in heaven at knowing that many saving and sanctifying ordinances can now be performed which will bless the lives of many. In speaking of temple work at the dedication of the Salt Lake Temple, President Wilford Woodruff declared, "There is a mighty work before this people. The eyes of the dead are upon us. This dedication is acceptable in the eyes of the Lord. The spirits on the other side rejoice far more than we do, because they know more than we do of what lies before the great work of God in this last dispensation . . ."[1]

There are countless numbers of spirits in heaven who have not yet had the saving and exalting ordinances of the gospel done for them. Until this work is completed, they cannot progress. Since this work can only be done on earth, it is understandable that heavenly spirits rejoice greatly when a temple is completed because it increases the likelihood of having their own ordinance work done.

When the corner stones for the Salt Lake Temple were laid, Parley P. Pratt commented that he felt that Joseph Smith and many angels were present. He told the audience the next day, that no one should wonder and marvel that angels would be at the ceremony surrounding a new temple, as heavenly beings had a great interest in temples. Parley added, "If they (angels) looked upon the earth at all, it would be upon those Corner Stones which we laid yesterday . . . It is here, that the spirit world would look with an intense interest, it is here that the nations of the dead, if I may so call them, would concentrate their hopes of ministration on the earth in their behalf. It is here that the countless millions of the spirit world would look for the ordinances of redemption . . ."[2]

As the following stories show, joyful angels often attend dedication services and sometimes show themselves because of their unrestrained happiness at seeing God's eternal purposes roll forward on the earth.

Kirtland Temple

When the Saints first lived in Kirtland, it was an unusually happy and peaceful time. The restored gospel was just beginning to move forward. The church had been formally organized, the Book of Mormon was published and men were being sent off to do missionary work. Through much sacrifice, the Saints constructed the first temple to be built in the latter days, the plans for which were revealed by an angel to the Prophet Joseph Smith. When the Kirtland Temple was dedicated on March 27, 1836, angels came to earth in one of the most grand and glorious spiritual outpourings ever encountered on earth.

At the end of the dedicatory prayer for the Kirtland temple, Joseph Smith declared, "And help us by the power of thy Spirit, that we may mingle our voices with those bright, shining seraphs around thy throne, with acclamations of praise, singing Hosanna to God and the Lamb!" (D&C 109:79)

Prescindia Kimball was among those privileged to see angels atop the Lord's temple. She states, "In Kirtland we enjoyed many very great blessings and often saw the power of God manifested. On one occasion I saw angels clothed in white walking upon the temple. It was during one of our monthly fast meetings, when the saints were in the temple worshipping. A little girl came to my door and in wonder called me out, exclaiming, 'The meeting is on the top of the meeting house!'

"I went to the door, and there I saw on the temple, angels clothed in white covering the roof from end to end. They seemed to be walking to and fro; they appeared and disappeared. The third time they appeared and disappeared before I realized that they were not mortal men. Each time in a moment they vanished, and their reappearance was the same. This was in broad daylight, in the afternoon. A number of the children in Kirtland saw the same. When the brethren and sisters came home in the evening, they told of the power of God manifesting in the temple that day . . . It was also said, in the interpretation of tongues, 'That the angels were resting down upon the house.'"

She continued, "At another fast meeting I was in the temple with my sister Zina. The whole of the congregation were on their knees, praying vocally, for such was the custom at the close of these meetings when Father Smith presided; yet there was no confusion; the voices of the congregation mingled softly together. While the congregation was thus praying, we both heard, from one corner of the room above our heads, a choir of angels singing most beautifully. They were invisible to us, but myriads of angelic voices seemed to be united in singing some song of Zion, and their sweet harmony filled the temple of God."[3]

On March 27, 1836, morning and afternoon services were held in the new temple, with an intermission of twenty minutes in between. During these meetings, hundreds of Saints witnessed various spiritual manifestations. One occurrence, which had countless witnesses, was the appearance of a tall angel.

One account of this experience stated; "During the ceremonies of the dedication an angel appeared and sat near President Joseph Smith, Sen. and Frederick G. Williams so that they had a fair view of his person. He was a very tall personage, black eyes, white hair and stoop shouldered, his garment was white, extending to near his ankles, on his feet he had sandals. [Joseph Smith stated that] He was sent as a messenger to accept of the dedication."[4]

Truman O. Angell was in the temple at the same time and relates; "When about midway during the prayer, there was a glorious sensation passed through the House; and we, having our heads bowed in prayer, felt a sensation very elevating to the soul. At the close of the prayer, F.G. Williams being in the upper west stand—Joseph being in the speaking stand next below—rose and testified that midway during the prayer an Holy Angel came and seated Himself in the stand. When the afternoon meeting assembled, Joseph, feeling very much elated, arose the first thing and said the Personage who had appeared in the morning was the Angel Peter come to accept the dedication."[5]

Another account reports; "F.G. Williams arose and testified that while the prayer was being offered, a personage came in and sat down between Father Smith and himself, and remained there during the prayer. He described his clothing and appearance. Joseph said that the personage was Jesus, as the dress described was that of our Savior, it being in some respects different to the clothing of the angels."[6]

Later in the evening, Joseph Smith met with the quorums of the church and gave them certain instructions. The prophet opened the meeting to those brethren who wished to speak and later documented the marvelous manifestations that followed.

Joseph recorded; "Brother George A. Smith arose and began to prophesy, when a noise was heard like the sound of a rushing mighty wind, which filled the Temple, and all the congregation simultaneously arose, being moved upon by an invisible power; many began to speak in tongues and prophesy; others saw glorious visions; and I beheld the Temple was filled with angels, which fact I declared to the congregation. The people of the neighborhood came running together (hearing an unusual sound within, and seeing a bright light like a pillar of fire resting upon the Temple), and were astonished at what was taking place. This continued until the meeting closed at eleven p.m. The number of official members present on this occasion was four hundred and sixteen."[7]

A solemn assembly took place soon after the House of the Lord had been dedicated. Brother Whitney attended this meeting and wrote in his journal; "The meeting continued on through the night, the spirit of prophecy was poured out upon the assembly, and cloven tongues of fire sat upon them; they were seen by many of the congregation. Also angels administered to many and also were seen by many. This continued several days and was attended by a marvelous spirit of prophecy."[8]

In the evening, the Prophet Joseph met with the presidency. All members, beginning with the eldest, received an anointing and blessing under the hands of Father Smith. After this round of blessings, Joseph testified, "The heavens were opened upon us, and I beheld the celestial kingdom of God, and the glory thereof, whether in the body or out I cannot tell. I saw the transcendent beauty of the gate through which the heirs of that kingdom will enter, which was like unto circling flames of fire; also the blazing throne of God, whereon was seated the Father and the Son.

"I saw the beautiful streets of that kingdom, which had the appearance of being paved with gold. I saw Fathers Adam and Abraham, and my father and mother, my brother, Alvin, that has long since slept, and marveled how it was that he had obtained an inheritance in that kingdom, seeing that he had departed this life before the Lord had set His hand to gather Israel the second time, and had not been baptized for the remission of sins . . . Many of my brethren who received the ordinance with me saw glorious visions also. Angels ministered unto them as well as to myself, and the power of the Highest rested upon us, the house was filled with the glory of God and we shouted 'Hosanna to God and the Lamb.'"[9]

The High Councilors of Kirtland were then invited into the room. They were also anointed and blessed by Father Smith. Joseph said, "The visions of heaven were opened to them also. Some of them saw the face of the Savior, and others were ministered unto by holy angels, and the spirit of prophecy and revelation was poured out in mighty power; and loud hosannahs, and glory to God in the highest, saluted the heavens, for we all communed with the heavenly host."[10]

In one of the more grand manifestations, the Prophet Joseph wrote that "President Zebedee Coltrin . . . saw the Savior extended before him as upon the cross, and a little after, crowned with glory upon his head above the brightness of the sun."[11]

On Friday, the 22nd, the brethren met again. The prophet said, "The heavens were opened, and angels ministered unto us." Joseph stated that after President Rigdon concluded the meeting with prayer, "angels mingled their voices with ours, while their presence was in our midst."[12]

Harrison Burgess wrote; "The Lord blessed His people abundantly in that Temple with the Spirit of prophecy, the ministering of angels, visions, etc. I will here relate a vision which was shown to me. It was near the close of the endowments. I was in a meeting for instruction in the upper part of the Temple, with about a hundred of the High Priests, Seventies and Elders . . . the spirit of God rested upon me in mighty power and I beheld the room lighted up with a peculiar light such as I had never seen before. It was soft and clear and . . . I beheld the Prophet Joseph and Hyrum Smith and Roger Orton enveloped in the light: Joseph exclaimed aloud, 'I behold the Savior, the Son of God.' Hyrum said, 'I behold the angels of heaven.'"[13]

The apostle George A. Smith testified that "On the evening after the dedication of the Temple, hundreds of the brethren received the administering of angels, saw the light and personages of angels, and bore testimony of it."[14]

Another time Elder George A. Smith spoke of the experiences in Kirtland and said, "That evening there was a collection of Elders, Priests, Teachers and Deacons, etc., amounting to four hundred and sixteen, gathered in the house; there were great manifestations of power, such as speaking in tongues, seeing visions, administrations of angels. Many individuals bore testimony that they saw angels, and David Whitmer bore testimony that he saw three angels passing up the south aisle, and there came a shock on the house like the sound of a mighty rushing wind . . ."[15]

Truman O. Angell, who later worked on building the Nauvoo Temple and after crossing the plains was called to be the architect for the church, recalled his experience with angels at the Kirtland Temple. He states, "Before closing this writing I desire to mention another important incident in connection with the Kirtland Temple. After the building was dedicated, a few of us (some six or eight) having Patriarch Joseph Smith, Sr. in company, went morning and evening to pray; entering at the West end of the Temple and going clear through to the East stand . . . One evening, having been in the country, I was too late to enter with the brethren; the company would not emerge til quite dark. I had tried the door and knew they were at prayer. I felt out of place and went to my house, but soon came out and met Brother Brigham Young out a little inquiring for Oliver Cowdery. I said I had not seen him. We walked toward the Temple approaching the building on the side which was used for the Prophet Joseph and His counselors . . . When about ten rods distant, we looked up and saw two Personages; one before each window, leaving and approaching each other like guards would do. This continued until quite dark. As they were walking back and forth, one turned his face to me for an instant but while they walked to and fro only a side view was visible. I have no doubt but the House was guarded; as I have no other way to account for it.[16]

Nauvoo Temple

Even before the Nauvoo Temple was completed, the Saints knew they would have to abandon it and leave their beloved city because of steadily increasing persecution. Plans were formulated for their exodus and although a few people were already leaving Nauvoo in November and December of 1845, the majority stayed behind, with many of them working feverishly to finish the temple. The beautiful white sandstone edifice was dedicated privately April 30, 1846, then dedicated publicly in sessions spanning the following three days. However, a small part of the temple had been dedicated in October of 1845 in order to allow people to receive their ordinances before fleeing the city. In December, Brigham Young was administering temple ordinances day and night, even while some Saints were escaping the city by crossing the frozen river.

Around the time of the temple's dedication, Nancy Naomi Alexander Tracy, along with others, witnessed a thrilling sight when they saw heavenly bands playing their music upon the top of the temple. Writing about conditions in Nauvoo just prior to the Saints' expulsion, Nancy says; "The spirit of enmity and hatred seemed to fill the hearts of the gentiles against us, but still the brethren continued the work on the temple determined to finish it. Ordinances were performed during the winter of 1845 and 1846 prior to the exit of the Saints from Illinois . . . We did not enjoy our beautiful city and temple very long. The temple was a fine structure to behold. I remember being aroused from my sleep one night by hearing such heavenly music. Everything was so still and quiet when it burst upon my ear. I could not at first imagine from what source it came. I got out of bed and looked out of the window toward the temple. There on the roof I saw the bands congregated and they were playing beautifully. The moon was shining brightly and the music was delightful."[17]

In his diary, John Pulsipher records, "The Saints gathered into Nauvoo, labored and toiled to finish the Temple . . . Most of the Saints, men and women, had the privilege of receiving their endowments, learning the order of the Priesthood, the fall and redemption of man, in the Temple. . . It was built according to the pattern that the Lord gave to Joseph. It was accepted of the Lord and His holy angels have ministered unto many therein and now because of persecution we must leave it and in leaving it we leave a monument of our industry which was reared, in our poverty. It was the finest building in all the western country."[18]

Samuel Whitney Richards had a remarkable vision in the Nauvoo temple. He writes; "Sunday, March 22nd, 1846. I went to my Seventies Quorum meeting in the Nauvoo Temple. The whole quorum being present consisting of fifteen members . . . Dressing ourselves in the order of the Priesthood we called upon the Lord, his spirit attended us, and the visions were opened to our view . . . there appeared a great company as it were of saints coming from the west . . . and I beheld other things which were glorious while the power of God rested down upon me. Others also beheld angels and the glory of God . . . Our joy increased by the gift of tongues and prophecy by which great things were spoken and made known to us."[19]

Manti Temple

When the Manti Temple was dedicated on May 21, 1888, the spiritual outpourings ranged from angelic singing, to bright lights, to appearances of spirit personages. Helen Mar Whitney, daughter of Heber C. Kimball, was a regular contributor to the *Woman's Exponent*—an independent newspaper—and wrote in one of her articles that angels are around us all the time and know everything that happens among the Latter-day Saint people.

She states; "This I believe to be verily true. It brought to my mind the testimony of many who were present at the dedication of the Manti Temple, whose eyes were opened, and they bore witness of many glorious visions, of personages who appeared to them with the heavenly music and singing, which was heard at different times, all proving that we are not separated from those who were co-workers with us here, and are still engaged in the interest of those with whom they labored for years in establishing the principles of this Gospel, and planning for the holy Temples, in which the work is continuing on for the living and for the dead."[20]

There were many accounts of heavenly music. Susannah Turner Robison attended the dedicatory services and related; "At the temple services to which I refer, many of us, probably all who were present, but many who were there I know, for we discussed the event afterward, heard an invisible choir singing. I looked around to see if I could discover from whence the music came, but I could see no one. The circumstance for the moment impressed me as being a very strange thing. The music was most beautiful, and seemed most heavenly. We all felt that it was a choir from the spirit world, singing the praises of the Lord in testimony of His approval and pleasure of the completion of another of His temples."[21]

Another account states; "On the 21st of May, before the opening exercises commenced, Brother A. C. Smythe, the chorister, seated himself at the organ, and rendered a piece of sacred music, a selection from Mendelssohn at the conclusion of which, persons sitting near the center of the hall, and also on the stand at the west end, heard most heavenly voices and singing—it sounded to them most angelic, and appeared to be behind and above them, and they turned their heads in the direction of the sound, wondering if there was another choir in some part of the temple.[22]

The Latter-day Saints *Millennial Star* added the following about the dedication services: ". . . A number of the Saints in the body of the hall and some of the brethren in the west stand heard most heavenly voices singing. It sounded to them as angelic, and appeared to be behind and above them, and many turned their heads in that direction wondering if there was not another choir in some other part of the building. There was no other choir, however, and nothing was transpiring but the concluding of the voluntary by Professor Smythe, and a little confusion in the body of the hall consequent upon the ushers seating the congregation."[23]

Another observer, John D.T. McAllister, declared; "In the Manti Temple the power of God was also manifested to a great degree. I was present at the dedicatory services. At the opening meeting in the upper main room, I heard what seemed to be a choir singing. The music was heavenly. I asked a brother on my left if there were any serenaders out-side. He said he knew of none. The sound came at first from the direc-tion of the southeast corner, and while President Lorenzo Snow was speaking from the upper stand they seemed to be behind and almost over him. I was thrilled with the music, the words I could not under-stand; the harmony was perfect. I said to myself, ' If Brother Snow heard that music he would not speak now.'"[24]

Many participants in the dedicatory services witnessed bright light surrounding church leaders. The following was reported in the *Millennial Star:* "On the 22nd of May, when Brother John W. Taylor was speaking, a bright halo surrounded him, and in that halo the per-sonages of Presidents Brigham Young, John Taylor, and a third person-age, whom she believed to be the Prophet Joseph, were seen by Sister Emma G. Bull of Salt Lake City; also the personage of Brother Jedediah M. Grant was seen by her standing by his son, Heber J. Grant, looking towards him while he was speaking; they were surrounded by a bright halo."[25]

A temple worker wrote the following in a published report; " . . . A bright halo was seen by Sisters Emma G. Bull, Ellen B. Matheny and Elizabeth H. Shipp, around Brothers John Henry Smith and Francis M. Lyman while they were speaking. On the 23rd the singing and voices were heard by a number of the members of the choir, and the halo of light was seen around Brothers John W. Taylor and Heber J. Grant by sisters Amelia F. Young and Elizabeth Folsom. I was sitting at the foot of the east stand, taking notes of the services; I looked up while Brother Heber J. Grant was speaking, and saw a bright halo surrounding him, which swayed to and fro as he moved his body. I laid down my pencil and gazed steadily at him for a few moments."[26]

Fourteen members of the church, in a signed statement, testified about their experiences. Part of their statement, which was published in the Deseret News, read: "A bright halo of light was seen by a number of persons over and around the heads of the following speakers—viz: Lorenzo Snow, Jacob Gates, Robert Campbell, John Henry Smith, Francis M. Lyman, John W. Taylor and A.M. Cannon. Brother Canute Peterson, of Ephraim (a very reliable and able man of affairs), observed this halo around the heads of all the speakers. While the public dedica-tory prayer was being offered by Brother Lorenzo Snow, near the mid-dle of the prayer, during a pause, the words, 'Hallelujah, hallelujah, the

Lord be praised' was uttered by a voice in a very soft and melodious tone, heard by brother Lewis Anderson, one of our assistant recorders here."[27]

M.F. Farnsworth, the temple recorder for the Manti temple, wrote the following for the *Millennial Star.* "Sister Rhoda W. Smith writes me the following under date of May 23, 1888. "The many manifestations of the holy Spirit that I saw and heard will never, no never be forgotten. When Apostle Lorenzo Snow arose, a beautiful heavenly light enveloped his head and shoulders; he looked angelic. In the same manner did the Holy Spirit fall on Brothers Wells, Lyman, Grant, and others that I did not know their names; particularly was the Spirit made manifest through Apostle John W. Taylor.

"When he first arose to speak, the same light surrounded him as it did the others; then a bright light, brighter than the noonday surrounded him, from the tips of the fingers on the right hand, up the arm, over the head and shoulders, and down the left arm; it was a glorious bright yellow light, and stood out from three to five inches wide, and the rays from the light formed a glorious soft halo of milky while light all around him.

"There was also a column of light receding obliquely from the back of his head toward the ceiling; it appeared like a beautiful bright sunbeam; his form was reflected on the wall behind, like the sunlight pouring into a closed room through a window; and when he was relating his vision at his father's deathbed there were two other bright reflections on the wall. I saw not the substance, but the bright reflections were there, and appeared to be reclining toward him; in fact he appeared to be transformed into a heavenly being, and it did not leave him when he took his seat or moved about the stand. I asked Sister Squire, who sat beside me, if she saw it. She said she saw the cloud of white vapor, but not the bright light. When Apostle Lyman was speaking, I heard strains of heavenly music coming from above; sometimes soft, sometimes louder, as though it might be a choir with music, wafting to and fro in the air."[28]

Departed church leaders were witnessed by some. Elder Franklin D. Richards, a member of the Council of the Twelve recorded the following; "When we dedicated the temple at Manti, many of the brethren and sisters saw the presence of spiritual beings, discernable only by the inward eye. The Prophets Joseph, Hyrum, Brigham and various other

Apostles that have gone, were seen, and not only this, but the ears of many of the faithful were touched, and they heard the music of the heavenly choir."[29]

Salt Lake Temple

Angels attended not only the dedication of the Salt Lake Temple but were also present when the corner stones were laid. On April 6, 1853, the First Presidency—along with the twelve apostles and other leaders—laid the corner stones. Parley P. Pratt spoke to the audience and declared that many angels were in attendance on that solemn occasion.

He stated, "It was not with my eyes, not with the power of actual vision, but by my intellect, by the natural faculties inherent in man, by the exercise of my reason, upon known principles, or by the power of the Spirit, that it appeared to me that Joseph Smith, and his associate spirits, the Latter-day Saints, hovered about us on the brink of that foundation, and with them all the angels and spirits from the other world, that might be permitted, or that were not too busy elsewhere." [30]

Standing near the north east corner stone, Parley continued speaking to the crowd. "Ye are assembled here today, and had laid these Corner Stones, for the express purpose that the living might hear from the dead, and that we may prepare a holy sanctuary where 'the people may seek unto their God, and for the living to hear from the dead, and that heaven and earth, and the world of spirits may commune together . . .'" [31]

On the 17th of April, 1893, the Salt Lake Temple was dedicated. The skies were heavy with storm clouds and rain beat down. Yet the glory of that day far outweighed the gloomy weather. Susa Young Gates said that it was her privilege to transcribe the official notes of the various meetings. At the official dedication, Susa was sitting on the lower side of the east pulpits, at the recorder's table. Just as President Joseph F. Smith stood to speak, Brother John Nicholson came in and sat down beside her.

She noted; "Almost as soon as President Smith began to address the Saints there shone through his countenance a radiant light that gave me a peculiar feeling. I thought that the clouds must have lifted, and that a stream of sunlight had lighted on the President's head. I turned to Brother Nicholson and whispered, 'What a singular effect of sunlight on the face of President Smith! Do look at it.'

"He whispered back, 'There is no sunshine outdoors—nothing but dark clouds and gloom.'

"I looked out of the window, and somewhat to my surprise, I saw that Brother Nicholson had spoken truth. There was not the slightest rift in the heavy, black clouds above the city; there was not a gleam of sunshine anywhere. Whence, then, came the light that still shone from the face of President Smith? Most people remember the terrible storm of that day. It was a day not easily to be forgotten. I was told afterwards by sister Edna Smith, who lived on the corner of First West and North Temple streets, that her parents came outside of their door at about the time of the opening of the services. They stood for some time watching the gloomy, cloud-swept heavens intently, when they saw all at once a glow of glorious light surround the Temple and circle about it as if it were an intelligible Presence.

"Later also, my sister, Carlie Young Cannon, who lived outside of the city, on what is known as the Cannon Farm, informed me that some members of her family came outside of their door on this same stormy morning. As they stood looking up toward the city, they, too, saw the strange light circling about the Temple walls. From their point of vantage they could see clearly that it was no effect of sunshine; for the clouds did not lift for an instant that day. Whence, then, came the light that shone from the face of President Smith? I was sure that I had seen the actual Presence of the Holy Spirit, focused upon the features of the beloved leader and prophet, Joseph F. Smith . . . I cherish the occurrence as one of the most sacred experiences of my life."[32]

Susa was not the only one to see the bright light. Brother Andrew Smith Jr., a member of the Tabernacle Choir, told his experience to John Nicholson who recorded it in the choir member's words. "President George Q. Cannon announced that a certain brother would read the dedicatory prayer. When he did so, I concluded that I would keep my eyes open and look at him, instead of closing them as I had done on previous occasions . . . A few moments after the Apostle began to read a scale seemed to remove from my eyes, and a bright light appeared above his head and behind him from his shoulders upwards. This light remained in that position a few moments and then raised until I could see the face of a personage in the midst of it. It was the countenance of President Brigham Young.

"I turned my gaze away for a moment, as if to ascertain whether I was looking with my own eyes. On again looking toward the stand I beheld the entire person of President Young, clothed in robes. He soon retired toward the rear of the stand and disappeared behind President Wilford Woodruff. After he had vanished I again turned my attention to the Elder who was reading, when I saw a light similar to what had appeared previously, and then I beheld the person of President John Taylor, who seemed to be looking towards the reader. I also saw a personage whom I took to be Hyrum Smith, although he appeared to be more spare in build than he is represented to be in his pictures; then Orson Pratt, whom I at once recognized; then there were three large men whom I could not identify.

"There were others of more slender build whom I also failed to recognize. There were, in all, about twelve whom I saw during the dedicatory prayer. When the prayer was concluded and just before and during the sacred hosanna shout, I noticed a bright halo of light surrounding several of the brethren, and the speakers during the same services were seemingly encircled by a brightness which appeared to emanate from their own persons.

"While President George Q. Cannon was making the concluding remarks during this session, I was overcome and wept for joy. Having my head bowed for a short time I saw nothing more for a few moments. On raising it again I saw a brilliant light over the head of each member of the First Presidency while they sat upon the stand. Whichever way any of the speakers turned while addressing the people, the light followed every movement made by them.

"The number of personages seen by me during the services subsequent to the reading of the dedicatory prayer was about twelve, making as near as I can state, about twenty-four in all. At the afternoon session on the same day I saw several personages, and immediately felt a desire to communicate the information of what I saw to Brother George Kirkman, who was sitting near me. The vision then became dim. I turned to him and told him of those appearances. On directing my gaze once more toward the Melchisedek stand, I could see nothing more, the vision having closed."[33]

Another interesting observation was printed in *The Contributor.* "President Joseph F. Smith was addressing the assemblage, which was very large. In all his previous speaking he had exhibited great power and freedom, the people being frequently melted to tears under the influence which accompanied his addresses. At this particular time, however, he appeared to have some difficulty in expressing himself with the ease and fluency that had hitherto characterized his utterances.

"One of the Elders who was standing on the Aaronic stand saw this and was looking intently at the speaker. As he did so he observed a light appear suddenly in front of the Melchisedek (sic) stand. This light was of a yellowish or golden tint and exceedingly brilliant. Its intensity was so great that, when in contact with the front pillars which support the canopy, it caused the white paint upon them appear of a dark hue. At the same instant of this appearance President Smith suddenly spoke with the same potent influence which had characterized his previous addressees, and continued to hold his audience as if they were spellbound, to the close of his remarks. The Elder referred to, learned that one other of the brethren besides himself had seen this manifestation of the Spirit of light."[34]

Speaking at the dedication of the temple, President Wilford Woodruff said, "I feel at liberty to reveal to this assembly this morning what has been revealed to me since we were here yesterday morning. If the veil could be taken from our eyes and we could see into the Spirit World, we would see that Joseph Smith, Brigham Young and John Taylor had gathered together every spirit that ever dwelt in the flesh in this Church since its organization. We would also see the faithful apostles and elders of the Nephites who dwelt in the flesh in the days of Jesus Christ. In that assembly we would also see Isaiah and every prophet and apostle that ever prophesied of the great work of God.

"In the midst of these spirits we would see the Son of God, the Savior, who presides and guides and controls the preparing of the kingdom of God on the earth and in heaven. From that body of spirits, when we shout 'Hosannah to God and the Lamb!' there is a mighty shout goes up of 'Glory to God in the Highest!' that the God of Israel has permitted His people to finish this Temple and prepare it for the great work that lies before the Latter-day Saints. These patriarchs and prophets who have wished for this day, rejoice in the Spirit World that the day has come when the Saints of the Most High God have had power to carry out this great mission."[35]

Although departed church leaders were occasionally seen during the dedication, some people saw angels they were related to. Jos. B. Keeler relates an experience that happened to a sister in his ward at the time of the dedication. Sister M. told Brother Keeler that to fully understand her story, it was necessary to know that her grandfather had three wives, two of whom died before her grandfather passed away. His last two wives had been sealed to other men and so were his only for this earth life. His first wife, whose name Sister M. did not even know, died in 1825. Sister M. attended the dedicatory services with her husband and recounted her experience as follows:

"While in that sacred place, we sat at a point between where the organ stood and the stand from which the brethren addressed the audience. I remember his telling the congregation to follow him closely and repeat the words as he went along. I closed my eyes and listened intently to his words. How long I had been thus listening I am unable to say; but just as one naturally falls to sleep, so I became unconscious of the things about me. Apparently I was not in the Temple, when lo! I found myself gazing at two persons standing in front of me—a man and a woman. The man I at once recognized as my grandfather, but the woman I did not know. It seemed the most natural thing in the world that I should meet them. Not the least thought of fear came upon me; on the contrary, I was happy to meet them, and they appeared to share similar feelings. They were dressed in white and both looked most heavenly. As I say, I did not know the woman; but she had dark hair, and was very beautiful indeed.

"Grandfather began talking to me, saying he wanted this lady sealed to him. His communication to me was not in our language, and I could hear no voice, although he made me clearly understand what he wanted, in a manner that I am unable to explain. The woman then asked me in a very earnest way to be baptized for her and to do her temple work; and further said, she wanted to be sealed to grandfather. Having seemingly finished their errand, they were apparently leaving, when grandfather turned partly around, and with a look which was meant to impress me, remarked, 'Remember, now remember!' His voice this time seemed audible. The scene then vanished. The words of the prayer now fell upon my ears and I listened as before. Three times after this, during the exercises, I felt what seemed to be a touch upon my arm and heard a voice say: 'Remember, now remember!' Yet I saw no one.

"The services over, we went slowly out of that sacred building. Just as I was on the last step of the stairway and the air from without fanned my face, I felt again that same touch on my arm. Unconsciously turning, I again heard that same voice, saying: 'Remember, now remember!' This time I felt weak and trembled from head to foot. My husband who had hold of my arm asked me if I was cold. Several sisters with whom we were talking as we came down the stairs also noticed my agitation, and asked me if I was chilly. I told them that I was not at all cold. While going home, I related this manifestation to my husband and remarked to him that I did not know who the woman could be or where I could ever get her genealogy so that I could do her work. Sometime after this occurrence, however, I was talking with my mother, and I found that her description of grandfather's first wife, so far as she knew it, agreed exactly with the appearance of the woman I had seen with him in the Temple. But how to get her name puzzled me for she was not my mother's mother.

"Shortly afterward mother and I ransacked her house in search of records, and finally we were rewarded by finding, down in the cellar, in a box of old newspapers, an almanac, on a blank leaf of which was a list of genealogies. Among them was the name of Harriet Fox—for one line of the record ran thus: 'Ezekiel Kellogg married Harriet Fox in 1818; she died about 1825.' This list had been prepared, so mother said, about twenty years ago by my grandmother at the request of a relative in the east who had written for genealogies, and a copy of it had been kept."[36] Sister M. went to the temple and performed the work that had been asked of her.

Adults were not the only ones to witness marvelous manifestations at the dedication of the Salt Lake Temple. An eleven-year old boy, George Monk, told his experience to John Nicholson who then recorded it as follows:

"He was at the dedication services accompanied by his mother and grandmother. He said he saw a man appear at the south-east circular window of the assembly hall of the Temple. This personage looked into the interior. The boy drew his mother's attention to this visitor but she could not see him. Suddenly he (George) requested her to look at two others flying or floating across the upper part of the hall from south to north, and then stated that five others had entered the large compartment and were ranged upon the wide ledge which runs along the wall under the row of circular windows. The lad was astonished to learn that his mother was unable to see any of those glorious personages, whom he described as the 'prettiest men' he ever saw in his life.

"At the conclusion of the services as soon as Elder John Henry Smith arose to pronounce the benediction the boy said in ecstasy: 'Mamma, look at that one under the clock, he is the prettiest of them all. See! He is holding up both his hands like this,' at the same time holding his own hands up as an illustration. This bright, innocent boy told his story by request, to several persons, it being each time similar in every detail. When on a visit to the Temple subsequently he pointed out the positions and movements of the eight personages as he saw them.

"Sister Monk corroborated, as far as could be done by her, in view of the fact that she was unable to see the angels herself, the statements of her son, who has the reputation of being a well-behaved and religiously inclined lad. The latter gave details as to the clothing of those holy beings, saying that they were dressed in loose flowing white robes. Most, if not all, had long and somewhat wavy hair. He was particularly struck with the great beauty of the one who stood over the canopy of the Melchisedek stand during the benediction, at the close of which he suddenly vanished from view."[37]

Another young boy, June Fullmer Andrew, had a similar experience. June was eight-years-old at the time of the dedication and his story has a fascinating ending. Brother Andrew said; "After the dedicatory prayer I beheld a beautiful choir dressed in dazzling white, singing hosannas to the Lord as they marched along the parapet of the temple. I turned to my parents and exclaimed to them how lovely the choir looked and how beautiful was their singing, for I was thrilled beyond measure. My parents told me the choir was not up there and were not singing, and they pointed out to me there was no room on the platform and that the parapet was not wide enough for people to march along it, so I was just imagining I saw them. I felt so squelched that I did not mention the incident again for many years, but I knew I had not been imagining.

"Many years later, when I was about forty years old, the authorities of the Church invited the High Priest and Seventy quorums and their wives of the Mount Ogden Stake to visit the Temple. The President of the Temple took us on a tour from the bottom to the top . . . He opened an east window near the top where we could view the parapet and showed us where the platform had been built and the dedicatory services had been held. I realized then that the choir I had seen and heard could not have been the Tabernacle Choir. After the tour we were assembled . . . for a testimony meeting. An Ogden lady, fifteen years my senior, arose to her feet and bore her testimony. She related being at the dedication of the Temple and explained how she had been thrilled with an angel choir which sang and marched about the parapet of the Temple, just as I had seen and heard them. When she finished I arose and confirmed what she had related as being true since I had experienced the same vision and acceptance of the Temple of the Lord."[38]

Notes for Part Ten

1 Wilford Woodruff, as quoted in *A Book of Remembrance, A Lesson Book for First Year Junior Genealogical Classes* (Salt Lake City: Genealogical Society of Utah, 1936), p. 82.

2 Parley P. Pratt, *Journal of Discourses,* vol. 1, p. 14.

3 Edward Tullidge, *The Women of Mormondom* (New York: 1877), pp. 207-208.

4 Helen Mar Whitney, "Life Incidents," *Woman's Exponent,* 1 February 1881, p. 130.

5 Truman O. Angell, "Stories of Yesteryear," *Our Pioneer Heritage,* compiled by Kate B. Carter (Salt Lake City: Utah Printing Co., 1967), p. 198.

6 *Lydia Knight's History, The First Book of the Noble Women's Lives Series* (Salt Lake City: Juvenile Instructor Office, 1883), p. 33.

7 Joseph Smith, *History of The Church of Jesus Christ of Latter-day Saints,* Period I, (Salt Lake City: Deseret News; 1904), p. 428.

8 Helen Mar Whitney, *Woman's Exponent,* vol. 9, no. 17, Feb. 1, 1881, p. 24.

9 Joseph Smith, *History of The Church of Jesus Christ of Latter-day Saints,* Period I, vol. II, (Salt Lake City: Deseret News; 1904), pp. 380-381.

10 *Ibid.,* p. 382.

11 *Ibid.,* p. 387.

12 *Ibid.*, p. 383.
13 Harrison Burgess, *Labors in the Vineyard, Twelfth Book of the Faith Promoting Series,* (Salt Lake City: Juvenile Instructor Office, 1884), p. 67.
14 George A. Smith, *Journal of Discourses,* vol. 2, p. 215.
15 George A. Smith, *Journal of Discourses,* vol. 11, p. 10.
16 Truman O. Angell, *Angell, Truman Osborn,* 1810-1887 (Salt Lake City: LDS Church Archives), pp. 10-11.
17 Nancy Naomi Alexander Tracy, *Diary of Nancy Naomi Alexander Tracy,* (Salt Lake City: LDS Church Archives), pp. 24-25.
18 John Pulsipher, as quoted by N.B. Lundwall in *Temples of the Most High* (Salt Lake City: N.B. Lundwall, 1941), p. 59.
19 Samuel Whitney Richards, as quoted by E. Cecil McGavin, *The Nauvoo Temple* (Salt Lake City: Deseret Book, 1962), pp. 50-51.
20 Helen Mar Whitney, *Woman's Exponent,* vol. 17, 15 October 1888, p. 73.
21 Susannah Turner Robison, as quoted by Jeremiah Stokes in *Modern Miracles* (Salt Lake: 1945), p. 136.
22 Francis M. Gibbons, *Lorenzo Snow, Spiritual Giant, Prophet of God,* (Salt Lake City: Deseret Book, 1982), pp. 186-87.
23 *Latter-day Saints' Millennial Star,* vol. 50, no. 26, p. 405.
24 John D.T. McAllister, "Temple Manifestations," *The Contributor,* vol. 16, January 1895, p. 147.
25 *Latter-day Saints' Millennial Star,* vol. 50, 13 August 1888, p. 522.
26 *Ibid.*
27 *Deseret News,* 30 May 1888.
28 M.F. Farnsworth, *Latter-day Saints' Millennial Star,* vol. 50, 13 August 1888, pp. 522-23.
29 "Genealogical and Temple Work," *Genealogical Magazine,* vol. 15, p. 148.
30 Parley P. Pratt, *Journal of Discourses,* vol. 1, p. 14.
31 Parley P. Pratt, *Journal of Discourses,* vol. 2, p. 145.
32 Susa Young Gates, "More Than a Halo," *Juvenile Instructor,* 15 November 1907, pp. 683-84.
33 *Ibid.*, pp. 116-117.
34 John Nicholson, "Temple Manifestations," *The Contributor,* vol. 16, 1895, p. 117.

35 Wilford Woodruff, as quoted in *A Book of Remembrance, A Lesson Book for First Year Junior Genealogical Classes, op cit.*, pp. 81-82.
36 Jos. B. Keeler, "A Wonderful Manifestation," *The Juvenile Instructor* vol. 3, January 1897, pp. 34-36.
37 John Nicholson, "Temple Manifestations," *The Contributor,* vol. 16, 1895, pp. 117-18.
38 June Fullmer Andrew, as quoted by Frederick & June Babbel, *To Him That Believeth* (Springville: Cedar Fort Incorporated, 1997), pp. 71-72.

Part Eleven
Angels Assisting
in Temple Work

The Lord sends angels to earth whenever there is a special work to be done that only a heavenly personage can accomplish. Because of the vast, eternal consequences of having the saving ordinances of the gospel done in the temple for our ancestors and the difficulty of obtaining correct genealogical records, angels are sometimes sent to assist in this all-important work. Elder Rulon S. Wells of the First Council of Seventy said, "The Lord has declared that He would bring to pass His wonderful work, and we know that He is doing so; that He has opened the heavens and sent messengers to the earth."[1]

There is a clear and unbreakable bond between us and our ancestors that is not broken by death. President Joseph F. Smith had strong feelings about the importance of temple work and spoke frequently on the subject, explaining that we are all part of a great family and need to be united with our ancestors. He said that was done by completing our genealogy and by seeing that the necessary temple ordinances for our loved ones were done.

During the eighty-sixth session of general conference, President Smith stated, "I believe we move and have our being in the presence of heavenly messengers and of heavenly beings. We are not separate from them. We begin to realize more and more fully, as we become acquainted with the principles of the Gospel, as they have been revealed anew in this dispensation, that we are closely related to our kindred, to our ancestors, to our friends and associates and co-laborers who have pre-ceded us into the spirit world. We can not forget them; we do not cease to love them; we always hold them in our hearts, in memory, and thus we are associated and united to them by ties that we can not break, that we can not dissolve or free ourselves from."[2]

Because of the unbreakable bond we have with our kindred dead, people who do temple work are often permitted to receive extra heav-enly inspiration and spiritual help. When conditions warrant divine aid, such help is given in accordance with God's plans. Elder John A. Widt-soe explains, "Many other intelligent beings superior to us, no doubt take part in the work of man on earth. There are angels and spirits who, no doubt, have assigned to them the care of the men and women who walk upon the earth. Man is not alone; he walks in the midst of such heavenly company, from whom he may expect help if he seeks it prop-erly and strongly."[3]

Although seeing an angel is rarely necessary, everyone has the right and privilege to receive inspiration and promptings to aid them in doing temple work. Joseph F. Smith said, "It is the right and privilege of every man, every woman and every child who has reached the years of accountability, to enjoy the spirit of revelation, and to be possessed of the spirit of inspiration in the discharge of their duties as members of the Church. It is the privilege of every individual member of the Church to have revelation for his own guidance, for the direction of his life and conduct."[4] All of the latter-day prophets have felt an urgency to do tem-ple work. Quoting Brigham Young, President Woodruff declared, "President Young has said to us, and it is verily so, if the dead could they would speak in language loud as ten thousand thunders, calling upon the servants of God to rise up and build Temples, magnify their calling and redeem their dead."[5] On another occasion President Woodruff said, "Let us try to live our religion, do our duty, and magnify our calling while we are here. The eyes of all heaven are over us. The eyes of the world are over us. The eyes of the angels are over us . . . When you get to the other side of the veil, if you have entered into these Temples and redeemed your progenitors by the ordinances of the House of God, you will hold the keys of their redemption from eternity to eternity. Do not neglect this! God bless you. Amen."[6]

Angels may whisper to a researcher where to find important records, overcome obstacles so that names are discovered, ensure that records are accurate, or assist in a hundred different ways to further temple work. As the following stories demonstrate, angels are very involved in temple work and sometimes motivate and prompt mortals to become similarly involved and work to accomplish this important task.

"You Will Find My Name in the Manti Temple"

Lorena Washburn Larsen had dedicated much of her life to searching out genealogical records and making sure temple work was done for her ancestors. Lorena worked tirelessly, researching and doing temple work and through the years, she had many special experiences. One of her sons, Enoch R. Larsen, recorded the following incident, where an angel appeared to Lorena.

"She (Lorena) very often would sit up late at night working for genealogy. Sometimes it would be two o'clock in the morning before she would get all of a certain line put down on the family group sheets before she could go to bed. One night after she had gone to bed and was asleep, she was awakened very suddenly—there by her bed stood two women. One of the women spoke to Mother and said, 'I am not a blood relative of yours, but I married one of your relatives. You will find my name in a Washburn book in the Manti Temple on page 54 about half way down the page.' Then she gave her name. The two women disappeared.

"Mother thought about this for a little while and then went back to sleep. A little while later Mother was awakened again and the same thing was repeated. After the two women had disappeared, Mother got out of bed and went downstairs and wrote all the details down on paper. Mother said she was sure it was a mistake because she had searched every Washburn book in the Manti Temple and there was not such a book there like the one the lady had described.

"About a month later, Mother went to the Manti Temple. Peter Poulson was the chief recorder there. Mother approached Brother Poulson and asked if she could see this certain Washburn book (which she knew was not there, and so Brother Poulson would say there was no such book there).

"Brother Poulson said, 'O.K. Sister Larsen—I was searching in the vault a week ago and I came to this Washburn book, and I thought you would like to see it, so I laid it aside for you when you came again.' He got the book and handed it to Mother. She was still doubtful as she turned to page 54. To her surprise, there she found it all as the woman had told Mother, and as she had written it down."[7]

"I Have Just Come from the Spirit World"

William Hurst spent part of 1892 and 1893 helping to paint the Salt Lake Temple. One evening, approximately four weeks before the temple was completed, he had two incredible, angelic visits, one from each of his two deceased brothers.

William recorded; "Along about March, 1893, I found myself alone in the dining room—all had gone to bed. I was sitting at the table when to my great surprise my old brother Alfred walked in sat down opposite me at the table and smiled. I said to him (he looked so natural): 'When did you arrive in Utah?' (He had lived in New Zealand and from whom I had not heard in years.)

"He said, 'I have just come from the Spirit World, this is not my body that you see, it is lying in the tomb. I want to tell you that when you were on your mission you told me many things about the Gospel, and the hereafter, and about the Spirit World being as real and tangible as the earth. I realized that you had told the truth. I attended the Mormon meetings.'

"He raised his hand and said with much warmth: 'I believe in the Lord Jesus Christ with all my heart. I believe in faith and repentance and baptism for the remission of sins, but that is as far as I can go. I look to you to do the work for me in the temple.' He continued: 'You can go to any kind of sectarian meeting in the Spirit World. All our kindred there knew you were trying to make up your mind to come and work on the temple. You are watched closely, every move you make is known there; and we were glad you came. We are all looking to you as our head in this great work. I want to tell you that there are a great many spirits who weep and mourn because they have relatives in the Church here who are careless and are doing nothing for them.'

"Three different times during our conversation I leaned over the table towards him and said, 'Alfred, you look, talk and act perfectly natural, it doesn't seem possible that you are dead.'

"And every time he replied, 'It is just my SPIRIT that you see, my body is in the grave.'

"There was a great deal more that he told me but these are the important items as I remember them. He arose and went out through the door he had entered.

"As I sat pondering upon what I had seen and heard, with my heart filled with thanks and gratitude to God, the door opened again and my brother Alexander walked in and sat down in the chair that Alfred had occupied. He had died in 1852 in New Zealand. I did the work for both he and Father in April, 1885. He had come from a different sphere, he looked more like an angel as his countenance was beautiful to look upon.

"With a very pleasant smile he said: 'Fred, I have come to thank you for doing my work for me; but you did not go quite far enough,' and he paused. Suddenly it was shown to me in large characters, 'NO MAN WITHOUT THE WOMAN AND NO WOMAN WITHOUT THE MAN IN THE LORD.'

"I looked at him and said, 'I think I understand, you want some person sealed to you.'

"He said, 'You are right, I don't need to interpret the scriptures to you but until that work is done I cannot advance another step.'

"I replied that the temple would be completed and dedicated in about 4 weeks and then I would attend to it as quickly as possible.

"'I know you will,' he said and then got up and left the room, leaving me full of joy, peace and happiness beyond description."[8]

A Voice in the Temple

While laboring together in the Logan temple, an aged mother and her son both heard angelic voices. In October of 1889, Patriarch Joseph Keddington and his mother were in the temple, performing ordinances on behalf of their dead relatives. While there, Sister Keddington heard a voice telling her that the names of her dead grandfather and grandmother were John and Elizabeth Hutchinson. This vital, new information allowed her to complete her genealogical line and do further ordinance work on behalf of her ancestors.

Joseph said that while there, he also heard a voice. The account states, "While he (Joseph) was engaged in receiving endowments for his dead uncle, John Barnes, he heard a voice saying, 'Your cousin, John William Tuckersfield, wants his work done!'"[9]

John had been working as a bricklayer when the platform he had been standing on collapsed, killing him. Before the fatal accident, Joseph had been teaching him about the gospel and his cousin had been very receptive towards it and was eager to hear more.

"We Have Been Waiting, Waiting, Waiting"

Bishop George Farnworth, had an amazing experience in July of 1888. Previous to the dedication of the Manti temple, George had pondered at length about his own ancestors and how the work could be done for them, as he had no records and no names. He was the only member of his family in the church and longed to know his ancestors. One day, shortly after the temple was dedicated, Bishop Farnworth left his home in Mount Pleasant and started for Manti. He writes:

"THE MORNING OF THE 16th OF JULY, 1888, about 10 o'clock while I was traveling between Pigeon Hollow and the Ephraim grave yard I felt a very strange sensation such as I never before experienced. Under this influence I went along and chancing to raise my eyes, it seemed that right in front of me there was a vast multitude of men; to the right and a little in front stood a large man about the size of my father, who weighed two hundred and forty-two pounds. This man waved his right hand towards the multitude and said: 'These are your kindred! And we have been waiting, waiting, waiting! Waiting for your temple to be finished. It is now dedicated and accepted by our Father. You are our representative, and we want you to do for us what we cannot do for ourselves. You have had the privilege of hearing the gospel of the Son of God; we had not that great blessing.'

"As he ceased, I looked at the great concourse and realized that they were all men, and thought it strange there were no women. I tried to recognize some of them but could not as I knew none. The thought came strongly into my mind, 'How can I find out their names, who and what they are?' Then a voice seemed to answer in my ears, 'When that will be required it will be made known.'

"I felt while looking at them, 'O shall I be worthy to help them?' whereupon I found tears were rolling down my cheeks and in the humility of soul I shouted, 'God help me!' adding aloud, 'God being my helper I will do all I can;' and it seemed as if the whole host shouted with one voice 'Amen!' I could stand it no longer, and cried aloud, while wiping my face and eyes. After I could control myself, I looked ahead and all had gone. During all this time, my team were going ahead at their own gait, but I had got no nearer to the multitude. Some of the men had white and some had dark clothes on. All their heads were uncovered."[10]

George felt so weak after this experience that he had to stop at a nearby house to rest. When he felt strong enough to travel, he went on to the temple and related his experience to President Wells. News of the angelic visit reached Brother Frank Farnsworth who worked as a recorder in the temple. Frank went to Bishop Farnworth and told him that while searching for his own genealogical line while overseas, he had found many people with the same name as the bishop. And although they were not his own ancestors, Frank felt compelled to gather their names.

"Now," Frank Farnsworth said, "You are welcome to these names for they are evidently your own kindred."[11] With a grateful heart, Bishop Farnworth took the names and with the help of his family, did the temple work for his ancestors.

They Had Not Yet Been Sealed

Sister Amanda H. Wilcox was in the temple, assisting in the ordinance of sealing children to their parents, when she saw an angel. On October 26, 1896, the record asserts that "Sister Amanda H. Wilcox saw the dead father of those children standing by the altar and he intimated to her that he and his wife, the mother of the children, had not yet been sealed."[12]

Sister Wilcox went immediately to President Winder, who was officiating, and notified him about the information the angel had given her. He immediately called a halt to the work. After a careful examination of the records, President Winder discovered that the angel was correct. The sealing had inadvertently been overlooked. Husband and wife were then sealed and afterwards, the children were sealed to their parents.

Sister Wilcox witnessed a special angelic visitation on another occasion. The record states; "Sister Amanda H. Wilcox, while in the morning meeting in the Temple Annex, saw a white curtain covering the windows on the stand, and a spirit personage came through an opening in the curtain and stood in front of the stand, affectionately gazing at the audience. Another manly spirit, glorious in appearance, held back the fold of the curtain and a number of women spirits entered and came to the front. The two men and all the women were dressed in beautiful white clothing. Sister Lenna Savage was then about to sing a solo and one of those women stood alongside of her, and joined with her in the singing. Sister Wilcox said, 'I understood that it was the dead mother of the girl who was singing.'

"When the song was finished, all of those spirit personages retired, except the man who had first entered. Sister Wilcox stated that she had frequently seen that same man, always dressed in white, in attendance in the annex, standing by the Recorders, and has seen him also in other rooms in the temple."[13]

Departed Parents Watch Children's Baptism

On February 20, in 1895, Sister Mary A. Schoenfelt was in the baptismal area of the temple when she saw two angels; a man and a woman. She was puzzled by their appearance and although she could see them quite clearly, did not recognize them. However, when Mary described them to her husband, he was able to identify them immediately.

The account says that Mary "saw the spirit persons of a man and woman, so clearly that she was able to minutely describe them to her husband, Edward Schoenfelt, when she returned home. He recognized the dead individuals by that description, and said they were his step-father's brother and the latter's wife for whom two of the Schoenfelt children were baptized that day."[14]

"Did You See Those Couples in the Room With Us?"

Bishop Joseph Warburton and his daughter, Emma M.W. Powell went to the Salt Lake Temple on December 1, 1898, to do sealing work for their ancestors. After they were finished, Joseph and Emma stepped over to President John R. Winder and told him how grateful they were that he had done the sealings for their family.

When they walked into the next room, Emma turned to her father and asked, "Did you see those three couples in the sealing room with us?

"His answer was, 'No, I did not.'

"She then said: 'There were three couples in the room. They were dressed in temple clothing, and the room was illumined by a supernatural light. As we knelt at the altar, and the names were called of the people for whom we were being sealed, each couple in turn knelt by our side. As the ordinance was performed they showed by the expression on their faces how pleased they were. When we walked up to thank President Winder, they came up also, and after we had completed our expression of thanks to him they disappeared.'

"Brother Warburton asked her if she could describe the people she saw. She replied she could do it very well, and she described each couple in turn.

"Her father then said, 'The first couple are my great-grandparents; the second couple my grandparents; and the third couple are my great uncle and aunt.' He had known them all in life, and from his daughter's description recognized them as the very persons for whom the sealings had been performed that day."[15]

A Silent Visitor

Minnie Scott had lost her husband less than a year previous to her encounter with an angel. With four small young children and a farm to run, Minnie usually fell into bed exhausted at the end of each day. One night however, the young widow lay down and briefly thought about the next day's chores before falling asleep. Suddenly, something startled Sister Scott and she awoke. A strange woman was standing at the foot of her bed. She had a coarse, heavy shawl around her shoulders and was holding out a white bundle toward Minnie. The stranger spoke not a word, but her sad eyes seemed to be begging for something. Then she was gone. Minnie pondered upon her silent visitor but eventually weariness overtook her and she fell asleep.

The account states, "The next night she (the woman with the shawl) appeared again, arms outstretched with a neatly-folded bundle of white. Her feet were wrapped in gunny sacks and she stood silently gazing with pleading eyes. The third night she came again and this time Sister Scott was unable to sleep after the little woman had left. She lay wondering who she might be and what she wanted.

"Early the next morning Sister Scott called her aunt who knew most everyone who had lived in that town since the early days. She had to know why she looked so unhappy and why she had come to her. As soon as she described the visitor to Aunt, she exclaimed; 'Oh, that's mother's sister. She came across in the Martin handcart Company and her feet were frozen so badly she could never wear shoes on her feet, but always kept them wrapped. I sure don't know why she'd be coming to see you, though, we had all the family's work done in the temple and all the children are sealed.'"[16]

Perplexed by this mystery, Minnie decided to carefully go over the genealogical records in her Book of Remembrance. In shock, she discovered that when the family had completed the ordinance work for their ancestors, her night-time visitor had been overlooked. While the woman's children had all been listed, her own name had been omitted. Sister Scott then realized that the white bundle the angel had held was neatly folded temple clothes and that she was appealing for someone to do her ordinance work in the temple. Sister Scott had the temple work done the following week and the silent visitor never returned.

"I Saw Thousands of Immortal Beings"

In 1881, Heber C. Kimball appeared to his son, David Patten Kimball, and told him that a great work was about to commence for the Kimball family in regard to temple work. From later events, it becomes evident that Heber was working mightily behind the veil to influence family members to research out names and do temple work for his ancestors.

In 1887, the Kimballs' held the first family reunion they'd had since Heber's death. Over three hundred relatives attended. One of Heber's sons, Solomon, stated, "We could feel the influence of our father working amongst us, and even those who were the most skeptic, could not help but acknowledge the hand of some unseen power operating in our midst."

Two years later, in 1889, Heber appeared to Solomon. In a letter written to his brother, Solomon wrote about seeing his father and the vision he'd had of the future. He said; "Night before last I had a glorious vision. I saw our father resurrected. He looked transparent and glorious to behold. I heard the most beautiful singing that I ever listened to, by hundreds of immortal beings. Many of our family and friends were present. It is a great comfort to me, and I am convinced that father will soon be resurrected. I also saw our elder brothers standing in the back ground, who seemed to have lost their places in the family, while the younger boys were taking the lead. I went to them and asked if they had any objection to my presiding over the meeting? They answered 'No,' and being next to them in age, I took charge. After the meeting was opened with prayer, I saw thousands of immortal beings, who made their appearance, and all sang in one grand chorus."[17]

Shortly after that vision, President Wilford Woodruff asked to meet with Solomon and set him apart as the designated leader of the Kimball family and told him to take charge of the temple work for his family.[18] At that time, temple work had only been done for seven of Solomon's relatives.

The feeling of urgency about completing temple work that his father had instilled into Solomon at the 1887 family reunion continued, although Solomon did not realize until years later the success his father was having on instilling that same genealogical spirit in other relatives. Although it was unknown to Solomon at the time, two distant relatives—one who was living in New Hampshire and the other in Massachusetts—felt prompted to begin doing genealogical research around the time of the 1887 reunion. Neither of them were LDS, yet they felt driven to search out their ancestors. For seven years they worked independently, having considerable success, yet remaining unaware of each other. They were also oblivious that Solomon was also working on his own in Salt Lake City.

After seven years of extensive, far-reaching work, the two relatives stumbled upon each other and discovered that each had been digging out names in the Kimball line. Happily, they joined efforts and combined their work. To their joy and amazement, they found their joint records totaled thirteen hundred pages and contained the names of nearly fourteen thousand ancestors. Shortly after, they learned about Solomon's efforts. They gave a copy of their records to Solomon, who shared the exciting news of this breakthrough with his family.

Solomon and his immediate family decided to hold a meeting in order to organize themselves to do temple work for their newly discovered ancestors. They decided to hold the meeting on the day of their father's birthday, June 14. On that day in 1897, they met at their private cemetery at the old Kimball Homestead on Main Street in Salt Lake City.

An unusual incident occurred that day, which Solomon recorded. "After we had commenced our services, I noticed an elderly gentleman standing on the outside, looking through the cemetery fence. He had a pleasant smile upon his countenance, and seemed much interested in what was taking place. The moment I noticed him, I experienced a thrill like unto an electric shock, which passed though my whole being, and caused me to leap for joy. Instantly I thought of the Scripture which says, 'Be not forgetful to entertain strangers, for thereby some have entertained angels unaware.' I immediately stepped up to the old gentleman and said: 'Come inside, stranger, you are welcome.'

"He politely bowed his head; walked around to the south side of the cemetery; passed though the gate, and sat down by my brother David, who presently came to me enquiring (sic) who the stranger was. He then told me of the heavenly influence that he experienced when the old gentleman sat down by him. Several others of the family spoke of the glorious sensation that they felt, when they came in contact with him. We could find no one who had ever seen him before, and none of us seemed to know when he appeared.

"His disappearance was just as mysterious as his coming, which caused me to wonder who this personage could be. Bishop Joseph Kimball thought that it was an angel who had been sent to take notes of our meeting . . . Some days after this meeting we commenced our work for the dead in earnest. Within seven years we were baptized for eleven thousand of our ancestors."

Solomon added, "Just previous to President Snow's death, I had a long talk with him upon this subject (temple work). He left the impression with me that he was in communication with my father and told me that father was around the temples, taking a great interest in the work for his kindred dead. He further said, that if my father's sons would become united and humble themselves before the Lord, that father would meet, and counsel with us just the same as he did when he was alive."[19]

"They Are Doing a Great Work for You"

James Gledhill saw firsthand the great joy that angels feel when their temple work is done. He relates the following experience; "Some time in November last, after having done considerable work in the Temple for my dead, I went to bed as usual, and lay meditating upon Temple Work. I heard the clock strike twelve, when my mind was led away, seemingly a long distance, to the foot of a very high mountain; but by what means I got there I do not know. I looked up the mountain as far as my eye could reach, and beheld, as if in another world, a multitude of people. A man came past me and went right in amongst the multitude, who were all very joyful.

"While I was looking wonderingly at the happy throng, I saw with unspeakable joy my father and mother near me, looking as they did when alive, only more pleased and happy. The man mentioned above seemed as he passed among the people to electrify them with joy. He said to a woman, 'I have come to let you people know that they are doing a great work down there for you.'

"'Down where?' she asked.

"'There is a place down there called Manti Temple,' he answered.

"'How do you know?' the woman asked; to which he answered, 'I have just come from there.' At this the woman broke into exclamations of joy and praise to God, in which the multitude joined.

"'I must go,' the messenger said, 'and let other people know.' They were unwilling to let him go; but he departed. The people appeared to increase immensely in number around the place where the information was received, until it seemed like an extensive valley filled with persons who were still gathering and rejoicing, and filling up the space as far as the eye could reach. . . . Then it appeared to me that I returned; but how I got back I knew not . . . I am now nearly eighty-two years old, and I write this (trusting you will publish it) in order to encourage my brethren and sisters in the great and grand work of redeeming the dead."[20]

Angels Assemble in the Temple

One evening, in February of 1886, the Logan Temple was flooded with light from the top spire down to the foundation. The account of this incident reads; "Apostle Marriner W. Merrill, who then was president of the Temple, observed the phenomenon as he was traveling on the highway that night from Logan to Richmond. It was likewise observed by many residents of Logan. No cause was found the next day.

"The following night, however, the Temple was again flooded with illumination, the same as the previous night. President Merrill announced to the general assembly in the Temple that this beautiful phenomenon was a spiritual manifestation. The matter was called to the attention of President Wilford Woodruff, who declared it to be an assembly of the great Hale family from the spirit World held in these sacred walls in exultation over their liberation through the beneficent ministrations in their behalf."[21]

"The Eyes of the Angels Are Over Us"

During his lifetime, President Wilford Woodruff continually urged members of the church to do temple work. He was well aware of how important it was to have these saving ordinances done, especially after a distinguished group of angels appeared to him and asked that their temple be done.

Relating this experience, President Woodruff states; "I feel to say little else to the Latter-day Saints wherever and whenever I have the opportunity of speaking to them, than to call upon them to build these Temples now under way, to hurry them up to completion. The dead will be after you, they will seek after you as they have after us in St. George. They called upon us, knowing that we held the keys and power to redeem them. I will here say, before closing, that two weeks before I left St. George, the spirits of the dead gathered around me, wanting to know why we did not redeem them.

"Said they, 'You have had the use of the Endowment House for a number of years, and yet nothing has ever been done for us. We laid the foundation of the government you now enjoy, and we never apostatized from it, but we remained true to it and were faithful to God.'"

President Woodruff then revealed who these special spirits were. He said, "These were the signers of the Declaration of Independence, and they waited on me for two days and two nights. I thought it very singular, that notwithstanding so much work had been done, and yet nothing had been done for them. The thought never entered my heart, from the fact, I suppose, that heretofore our minds were reaching after our more immediate friends and relatives."[22]

President Woodruff asserted that the forefathers of the United States were extraordinary men, declaring, " . . . those men who laid the foundation of this American government and signed the Declaration of Independence were the best spirits the God of heaven could find on the face of the earth. They were choice spirits, not wicked men. General Washington and all the men that labored for the purpose were inspired of the Lord."[23]

After being visited by these angels, President Woodruff took immediate action. "I straightway went into the baptismal font and called upon brother McCallister to baptize me for the signers of the Declaration of Independence, and fifty other eminent men, making one hundred in all, including John Wesley, Columbus, and others; I then baptized him for every President of the United States, except three; and when their cause is just, somebody will do the work for them."[24]

After the baptisms, President Woodruff arranged to have other ordinances done. He said during conference, "Brother McAllister baptized me for all those men, and then I told those brethren (J.D.T. McAllister, David H. Cannon and James G. Bleak) that it was their duty to go into the Temple and labor until they had got endowments for all of them. They did it."[25]

The Voices Repeated the Words of the Prayer

In the Salt Lake Temple, on July 20, 1893, a woman saw angels in a spiritual prayer circle. They were hovering above the brethren and sisters who were conducting a prayer circle. The report states that she "heard their voices repeating the words of the prayer that was then being uttered. A sister, who was with her, heard the spirit voices also, but she did not see the personages in the spirit circle."[26]

Notes for Part Eleven

1   Rulon S. Wells, *Conference Report,* April 9, 1905, p. 56.

2   Joseph F. Smith, *Conference Report,* April 1916, pp. 2-3.

3   John A. Widtsoe, *A Rational Theology,* seventh edition, (Salt Lake City: Deseret Book Company, 1965), p. 68.

4   Joseph F. Smith, *Conference Report,* April 1912, p. 5.

5   Wilford Woodruff, *Journal of Discourses,* vol. 19, p. 229.

6   Wilford Woodruff, *Conference Reports, op cit.,* p. 90.

7   Enoch R. Larsen, arranged by Floy L. Turner, Lorena Eugenia Washburn Larsen, *A Mother in Israel,* (Salt Lake City: Church Historian's Office Library), p. 70.

8   *Diary of Frederick William Hurst,* Compiled by Samuel H. and Ida Hurst, (Salt Lake City: LDS Church History Library), pp. 204-05.

9   *A Book of Remembrance, A Lesson Book for First Year Junior Genealogical Classes,* (Genealogical Society of Utah, 1936), p. 79.

10   "A String of Pearls for Those Who Have Intelligence to Appreciate Them," *Young Woman's Journal,* vol. 1, pp. 214-15.

11   *Ibid.,* p. 215.

12   *A Book of Remembrance, A Lesson Book for First Year Junior Genealogical Classes, op cit.,* p. 78.

13   *Ibid.,* p. 79.

14   Joseph Heinerman, *Temple Manifestations* (Manti: Mountain Valley Publishers, 1974), p. 127.

15   *A Book of Remembrance, A Lesson Book for First Year Junior Genealogical Classes, op cit.,* pp. 77-78.

16   Minnie Scott, as told to Jennis R. Farley (unpublished manuscript in possession of Ruth Gregory, Smithfield, Utah).

17   Solomon Kimball, *Thrilling Experiences* (Salt Lake City: Salt Lake City Magazine Printing Co., 1909), pp. 61-67.

18   At that time, it was common practice for the leaders of the church, after a patriarch had passed away, to call upon a worthy family member to take charge of seeing that research was done and temple work completed for the family's relatives. Since Solomon's older brothers were not fully active, Solomon was called upon to see that temple work for the Kimball family was done.

19 *Ibid.*, pp. 65-67.
20 *The Deseret News Weekly* vol. 38, 29 December 1888, pp. 28-29.
21 Jonathan Hale, as quoted by Joseph Heinerman in *Temple Manifestations* (Manti: Mountain Valley Publishers, 1974), pp. 170-71.
22 Wilford Woodruff, *Journal of Discourses,* vol. 19, p. 229.
23 Wilford Woodruff, *Conference Reports,* April 1898, p. 89.
24 Wilford Woodruff, *Journal of Discourses,* vol. 19, p. 229.
25 Wilford Woodruff, *Conference Reports, op cit.,* p. 90.
26 *A Book of Remembrance, A Lesson Book for First Year Junior Genealogical Classes, op cit.,* p. 78.

Index